"It happens,"
Luke said curtly

His callous words cracked Marion's professional armor.

Her voice was low but vibrant with anger as she blazed at him. "It happens. Is that all you can say? Don't you ever see your patients as human beings— or are they all just cases to you?"

It was an outrageous way for her to speak— unprofessional and unheard of.

The steel in Luke's eyes cut across the flood. "Emotion is a handicap," he said. "If you become personally involved it spells disaster for both you and the patient. With your experience I expected you'd have learned that, Sister Rowley."

Sister Rowley. Not Marion. It was like a slap in the face—a deliberate and demoralizing snub. Emotion is a handicap. So is being a woman, Marion told herself bitterly.

Angela Carson is a recent addition to Harlequin
Romance writers, and the quality of her writing
and her interesting characters will attract many
readers. She lives in the countryside near
Birmingham, England, where as well as writing
she is able to indulge her love of gardening.

Books by Angela Carson

HARLEQUIN ROMANCE
2317—THE VITAL SPARK
2619—THE FACE OF THE STRANGER
2853—GATHERING OF EAGLES

Sweet Illusion

Angela Carson

Harlequin Books

TORONTO • NEW YORK • LONDON
AMSTERDAM • PARIS • SYDNEY • HAMBURG
STOCKHOLM • ATHENS • TOKYO • MILAN

Original hardcover edition published in 1989
by Mills & Boon Limited

ISBN 0-373-03044-4

Harlequin Romance first edition April 1990

CHAPTER ONE

WHEEEP! Wheeep! Wheeeeep!

The buzzer in Marion's top pocket shrieked the high-pitched signal specially reserved for members of the mobile medical emergency team, or the Flying Squad, as they were irreverently known by Farnmere's hard-worked General Hospital.

In a well-rehearsed manoeuvre, several things happened at once.

A colleague appeared at Marion's side to take over the task on which she was engaged; her own hand reached up to press the answer button to let the switchboard know she had got their message and was on her way, and her feet sped her in the direction of the Casualty department's wide swing exit doors.

Without pausing, she called out to the receptionist, 'Ring Sue for me, will you, and tell her I might be late?'

The girl's cheery, 'Will do,' followed her as she reached the doors and put out both hands to push them wide and hasten her exit.

Another hand, at the end of a long, tanned arm, forestalled her, and swung the doors wide, and her own hands met fresh air instead of the expected resistance of heavy wood, and Marion's exit was considerably more hasty than she had intended.

Unbalanced by the suddenly unbarred exit, her speeding feet stumbled, and she would have fallen had not two hands come out and grabbed her with bruising strength, and dumped her unceremoniously back on to her feet again, while their owner criticised curtly, 'You

haven't got time to stop and rearrange your evening date.
Seconds count.'

As if she did not know, and his criticism was totally
unjustified, because she had not even slowed down to
speak, let alone stopped, but Marion had got no breath
left to reply as her rescuer's one hand retained its hold
on her arm, and he pulled her along with him at lung-
taxing speed towards the specially adapted, long-
wheelbase Range Rover that was already drawing out of
the garage in response to the same warning, and making
its way across the tarmac space between the garage and
the hospital gates, which was always kept clear for just
such emergency turnouts.

The fact that the mobile operating theatre-cum-
accident unit achieved those turnouts in two minutes flat
was a matter for pride at the General, but no matter
what the crew achieved in the way of performance,
nothing satisfied the impossible standards of Luke
Challoner.

Surgeon *extraordinaire*, and champion of the town's
need for a mobile emergency unit that took the hospital
to the patient when the highly trained crews of the ordinary ambulances judged a situation to be beyond their
own powers to deal with, Luke Challoner drove himself
as hard as he drove his crew.

The hospital board did not share his view as to the
overriding need for such a facility in the small but busy
market town of Farnmere, and in the teeth of their opposition Luke Challoner set out to prove them wrong.

They argued that the thirty thousand pounds plus
spent on buying and equipping the vehicle, to say nothing
of the cost of salaries for its crew, could be better spent
elsewhere, when the specialist facility would probably
only be needed once or twice a week.

Luke Challoner's answer came in the form of a train
derailment which sent him crawling in among the

wreckage at dire risk to himself to reach the trapped victims, many of whom he afterwards declared publicly would have been saved much suffering if such on-the-spot facilities had been available to them at the time.

Without scruple, he had used the media to back his cause, and the black-haired man with the brilliant blue eyes and the crooked smile, caused by a scarred lip, his own personal souvenir of the train crash, that saved his patient and injured himself, soon became a familiar figure in the local news.

Driven into a corner by public concern but still fighting back, the hospital board had given him a year to prove his point, which he seemed to be intent upon doing no matter what the cost to himself.

Or to his crew, Marion reflected ruefully, as the driver, himself a paramedic, honed to a high degree of skill by Luke Challoner in person, slowed the vehicle to a crawl and snapped open the door for them to jump on board.

Before the vehicle could brake to a halt, Marion found herself swung off her still running feet, and lifted bodily up into the high bench seat beside the driver, and she scarcely had time for the thought to track across her mind, Thank goodness none of us is fat, or there wouldn't be room, before Luke Challoner swung himself up beside her, and slammed the door shut with a brief, 'OK, Bill. Move.'

The surgeon's spare frame did not carry a surplus ounce, and it made a hard landing for Marion's slight figure as Bill obeyed his instructions with the finesse of a racing driver, and swung the big vehicle out of the hospital gates with its headlights full on, its top light flashing and its screaming siren cutting a right of way through the early afternoon traffic.

It straightened, and Marion picked herself hastily off the surgeon's shoulder, and blamed her racing pulse on the emergency that, in spite of the hours of remorseless practice upon which he insisted, never ceased to set the adrenalin flowing each time they were called out to a real case, made worse by the fact that until they reached the scene of the trouble she had nothing whatever to do except sit still and wait. Her copper curls were like a bright candle flame between the two men, and her green eyes seriously intent as she marvelled at the ability of their driver to achieve such high speeds without the slightest disconcertment to any other motorist on the narrow streets, steep and cobbled, and totally unsuited to twentieth-century traffic.

No one spoke. Bill was much too occupied in getting them to wherever they were going with the least possible loss of time to welcome the distraction of small talk, and Luke Challoner seemed to feel no need for friendly exchanges, and leaned forward to touch a switch on the dashboard in front of him and ask briefly as the special line to the hospital switchboard buzzed, 'Have you got any details for us? Give me the gen.'

'There isn't much yet, Mr Challoner. All we know so far is that a minibus has skidded off the road into a lamppost. The driver and passengers are all trapped inside. According to the ambulance crew who called you out, several of them seem to be badly hurt. They're standing by until you arrive. The fire brigade is on its way with cutting equipment. I'll buzz you if we hear more.'

The surgeon switched off and grunted. 'Humph. It's probably a party of youngsters out joy-riding. The winter's hardly started yet. What'll it be like by Christmas?'

How did he know who the victims were, or what they had been doing? Marion cast him a glance of pure dislike. They might not be youngsters. They could be senior citizens, on an outing from their day centre. And if they *were* young, who was he to criticise them? He could not be all that old himself. Marion judged him to be in his early thirties. The coal-black, springy hair held not a trace of grey, and his step bore the athletic spring of a man in his prime.

Luke Challoner was a fine surgeon, and a dedicated and caring medical man. But there, Marion thought, his good points ceased. As a man—an individual—he was hard all through. As hard and unyielding as the tanned, sinewy arm lying against her own along the seat, sending urgent prickles across her skin, making the tiny fine hairs stand up on goose pimples. Abruptly Marion pulled her arm away and laid it across her lap instead, breaking the electric contact with him, and then had to pull her eyes away from his face with even more haste as Luke Challoner turned his head and looked right back at her, registering but supremely indifferent to her withdrawal.

He seemed to have a sixth sense about other people's reactions to him, Marion thought uncomfortably. She had noticed it in action before. It enabled him to keep one step ahead whenever he happened to be at variance with someone else's point of view, which if her own experience of his abrasive manner was anything to go by must be pretty often.

At least they each knew where the other stood, she reflected, which was strictly on the opposite sides of the fence. Her own dislike of Luke Challoner was matched only by his total disapproval of her, a disapproval occasioned not by her impressive professional track record, which she was confident he could not fault, but by sheer irrational prejudice. He wanted an all-male crew on the Flying Squad, and she happened to be a woman.

Sexist! A frown marred her forehead as she remembered their brief but fiery interview just over a month ago.

Her own sense of fairness had to admit that Luke Challoner had a good reason for his stance. When his brain child had only just been launched, and he was forced to prove its success or climb down and admit defeat to the hospital board, which Marion judged he would die rather than do, the nursing sister who was working with him at the time had declared herself to be pregnant.

The girl's reaction to the early weeks of her first pregnancy made her less than fit to cope with emergency calls of the stressful nature encountered by the Flying Squad, and Luke Challoner had no hesitation in returning her to the wards at a speed which suggested she had committed some sort of crime.

His crusade was of more importance to him than people's feelings. Marion condemned him, not altogether fairly.

In the event, there was no time to place advertisements and conduct lengthy interviews. He needed an on-the-spot replacement and sent an SOS for one to the accident hospital in the nearby city, in response to which Marion arrived in his office the next day.

'I told them to send me a man,' was his curt unwelcome.

Told, not asked. The fiery spirit which matched the bright colour of Marion's hair rose at the rebuff.

'There isn't a man available with the qualifications you wanted,' she retorted.

Her own qualifications were ideally suited to cope with what her profession laconically termed trauma, and they gave her the confidence to stand up to this unreasonable, chauvinistic male, whose attitude was clearly meant to intimidate her.

To demonstrate its failure, Marion trotted out her attributes with businesslike crispness. 'Midwifery. Operating theatre. Intensive care. Casualty department.' It added up to an impressive list of experience of coping with major crises which, simply because she happened to be a woman, signally failed to impress Luke Challoner.

'Women! They snarl up everything,' he muttered. His voice was a snarl, and Marion's wrath rose.

'Having a baby involves a man as well as a woman,' she pointed out sweetly, and added as a reluctant after-thought, 'sir.'

Luke Challoner's black brows drew together over eyes that were a disconcerting gentian-blue, and pinpointed Marion with a steely look.

'That's another habit you'll have to get out of, Sister Rowley,' he shot back. 'The Flying Squad has got no time to bother with unnecessary formalities. For speed's sake we all use first names. Mine is Luke. Yours, I gather, is Marion. The driver is Bill.'

He had to consult the introductory note which Marion had brought with her from the accident hospital before he recalled her name, and his tone said she must not take the offer of his own first name as a concession to any personal friendliness towards herself.

That suits me fine, Marion fumed inwardly. Anything less likely than friendship with Luke Challoner would be hard to imagine. Luke. Mentally she erased his surname. No matter how difficult it might be for her to get into the habit of calling and thinking of him as Luke, she must school herself to do so or risk his instant criticism.

'That makes sense—Luke,' she answered deliberately, and held his look with a cool regard that turned her green glance to ice.

His eyes levelled with hers, and she blinked at his sharp qualification, 'It may not be necessary for long. The accident hospital still has my order for a suitably qualified male nurse to be a *permanent* crew member.'

His order. Like for groceries. Clearly, when he received delivery, he intended to return her, Marion, to where she came from, as swiftly, and with as little scruple, as he had got rid of her predecessor.

Marion's eyes snapped, but before she could speak he compounded his offence by commenting, 'So in the meantime don't you, too, decide to start having a baby.'

His bluntness was unforgivable even between members of the medical profession, and hard breath hissed through Marion's teeth as he went on before her heated mind could formulate a suitably cutting reply.

'Just thought I'd warn you. Wedding rings aren't always regarded as a necessary requisite nowadays.'

His glance swept across her ringless left hand, and lifted to mock the flood of colour which stained the fine skin of her face, so often the accompaniment to richly auburn hair.

Marion stared back at him, speechless with indignation. How dared he? How...

The desk telephone stopped her voice from hurling the words, and his job, back into his dark, sardonic face. The instrument's clamour diverted his attention, and he reached out to pick up the receiver, and gestured with his other hand towards the office door with the curt instruction to Marion, 'Report to Casualty. They'll kit you out with your uniform, and give you something to occupy you between calls. Yes? Challoner here.'

He spoke into the telephone mouthpiece, effectively cutting himself off from Marion, dismissing her from his mind as imperiously as he had dismissed her from the room.

There was nothing else she could do but obey him. Marion resisted an almost overwhelming temptation to slam the office door hard behind her, and leaned against the outside of it, fighting to regain her composure before she sought out the sister in charge of the Casualty department, in which she was to work in between calls for the Flying Squad.

'You look as if you've just bumped into the redoubtable Luke,' a laughing voice guessed accurately.

Its owner grinned, and Marion warmed to merry brown eyes that belied the touch of grey in the close-cropped hair underneath the lace cap. The newcomer invited, 'Come and have a cup of tea in my office and recover. I'm Sister in charge of Casualty, by the way. Joy, to you,' she added minutes later as she produced a tin of biscuits and a well used teapot, and began to pour out.

She handed a filled cup to Marion and grimaced. 'There's not been much joy here just lately, I'm afraid. Losing the other girl back to the wards has made us short-staffed. You're the most welcome sight I've seen today. Even although you'll only be filling in time between calls, every extra pair of hands is a help.'

'I'm glad someone thinks I'm welcome.'

The implication was obvious, and Joy's face sobered. 'You can't blame Mr Challoner for wanting a man, after what happened. He's had an uphill fight to get the Flying Squad on the road at all, and the battle to keep it there isn't over yet. Another setback might weight the scales on the side of the hospital board, and he can't risk that. What he says makes sense.'

'It isn't what he says, it's the way he says it that I object to.'

Joy laughed. 'He can be a bit abrasive at times, I admit, but you'll get used to his manner. He's a perfec-tionist in his work, which is all to the good so far as his patients are concerned, and he's gentleness itself with them.'

'That I've yet to see.'

'Don't judge him too harshly until you have. In the meantime, come and get your uniform. It's the one that was made for the other girl, but from the look of it you're about the same build, so it should fit. How do you like it?'

She held up dark blue trousers and a white tunic amply supplied with pockets, and turned it round the other way to show Marion the large red cross emblazoned right across the back.

Her eyes widened. 'It's distinctive, to say the least. It looks like a field-ambulance uniform.'

'Field ambulance more or less describes the sort of work you'll be doing. Mr Challoner had the uniform specially designed. He wears one like it himself as well. He's never forgotten the experience of crawling about among those damaged railway coaches, and the police mistaking him for an injured passenger and trying to pull him out before they rescued his patient. Anyone wearing this can be identified at a glance. It's the envy of the rest of the girls on the staff,' Joy teased.

'Anyone wearing this could be picked out at a hundred yards in the dark.'

'After dark you'll wear a slip-on fluorescent jacket in the same pattern, so that you can be seen. Put your uniform on, and then come and meet the rest of the staff in Casualty. You'd better look slippy, because I've no doubt Luke-the-lad will be whistling you up for a practice session any minute now, to get you into the feel of things as quick as maybe. He doesn't let the grass grow under his feet, nor under the feet of his staff,' she warned darkly.

Her all-too-accurate prophecy set the tone for the days that were to follow.

Marion hardly had time to drop her belongings into the locker allocated to her in the staff changing-room and don the Flying Squad uniform when the pocket buzzer supplied with it wailed its first summons.

What to do? Which way to go? Did Luke Chall...no, just plain Luke. Did he expect her to know these things as if by some sixth sense? Marion stood transfixed in the middle of the Casualty department.

She saw Joy start to hurry towards her, but Luke exploded from his office and got there first. He took

Marion by the elbow in a hard grasp, and his now familiar voice gravelled, 'Speed is of the essence. Don't just stand there. Come on.'

Marion was well accustomed to moving at speed, but this man seemed to be jet-propelled. Twice and often three times a day he called the team out on practice sessions, and each time with uncanny accuracy he managed to choose times which caused Marion the maximum inconvenience.

He seemed to take a malicious pleasure in ejecting her from the ladies' loo. Several times she had to abandon her much-needed meal breaks, and one morning he caught her half dressed in the act of changing into her uniform.

She had come in specially early to give herself time to put it on and do up the buttons in peace, in a bid to foil his unremitting demands upon every second of her time, and when they reached the Range Rover, his searing reference to the one button left undone, in a position that scarcely mattered anyhow, left her smarting and angry.

After that, she came ready dressed in the uniform, and carried a spare with her in case the one she wore became soiled during the day, but even that did not prevent Luke from finding other ways of testing her.

His constant criticisms flicked her on the raw, but they had the effect of putting her on her mettle so that in self-defence she began to anticipate every move he might demand of her in order to stem his comments at source.

The pace at which he drove her amounted almost to mental cruelty, but if he hoped to break her, as opposed to breaking her in to the ways of his team, he was way off course, Marion fulminated. Her experiences of the last few years had not produced a quitter. She had spent them in battling to bring up her small son single-handed, and working to earn sufficient money to keep a roof over their heads after the oil-rig accident that left her a widow even before her child came into the world.

At no small cost to herself she won through, but the experience toughened her mentally and physically, and she was prepared to fight even harder to keep her job at the General.

She needed work in Farnmere itself now, just as much as Luke needed an assistant, but cautiously she kept that particular piece of information to herself.

Her need was her Achilles' heel, and she had no intention of exposing it to the hard, uncaring eyes of Luke Challoner, who would no doubt use it as a whip with which to belabour her, and would become even more difficult to work with, if that were possible, than he was already.

And so Marion remained discreetly silent on personal issues, just as she omitted to explain her ringless left hand. It had become a casualty of her need to cope alone. One day, tackling a do-it-yourself chore with more vigour than expertise, she hit her hand hard with a hammer instead of the nail she aimed at, and the resulting damage to her finger forced the hospital to cut off her wedding ring.

The finger healed slightly misshapen, and when a local jeweller returned the ring to its original circle, it was too small to slip over the enlarged knuckle joint, and so Marion wore it on a chain round her neck, tucked out of sight under the high collar of her uniform.

She was secure in the knowledge that Luke had no means of finding out anything about her personal life. Her CV which accompanied the letter of introduction from the accident hospital gave only her career path, and her professional title of Sister, not her married status, and she saw no reason to impart information that was no concern of his.

If he had been more human in his approach she might have felt constrained to tell him that, now five years old, Robbie was due to start school at the beginning of the autumn term, and she needed to find work in the town itself instead of at the accident hospital in the city several miles away. Until now, she had been able to take Robbie with her daily to be cared for in the hospital crèche, a facility much appreciated by the working mothers on the staff.

The job at the General seemed like an answer to her prayer.

True to her promise, Sue, her next-door neighbour, took Robbie to school each morning with her own twins of the same age and collected him each evening, and if Marion expected to be late home, a telephone call from the receptionist in Casualty was all that was needed to ensure that Robbie would be fed and looked after until Marion was able to return and take charge.

Work with the Flying Squad proved to be all that Luke predicted, and more. Nothing in Marion's previous experience had prepared her for the extreme mental and physical pressure placed on her by each new turnout.

Now, she learned the reason for those endless, exasperating practice sessions, with Luke's voice always goading her, driving her to further and further efforts. Honing her, she now acknowledged reluctantly, to that sharp edge of perfection which was the crew's strongest weapon against that final, dark *force majeure* that hovered over each new call for their help.

Once away from the hospital, they were on their own. There were no other skilled hands reaching out to help them. No more facilities than those they carried in the admittedly superbly equipped Range Rover. Only each other, and the implacable discipline wielded by Luke, that welded them together like cogs in a well-oiled machine.

Multiple road crashes, heart attacks, several bad motorcycle accidents, and a gas explosion later, to say nothing of a major fire and a caved-in trench that was being dug out to lay a new sewer, and instead nearly buried the diggers, Marion had cause to be grateful for her now automatic anticipation of Luke's every need.

She had cultivated the habit for a very different reason, but she found the result invaluable as she crawled beside Luke through tangled wreckage or blinding smoke, able to be in the exact spot, at the exact second, to do just the one thing he wanted, without his having to wait or to tell her what to do, a dire necessity in situations where speech was frequently rendered inaudible by surrounding uproar.

Once, and only once, Luke came near to thanking her for her help.

It had been a particularly dangerous assignment. To reach the patient, they had to crawl under an upturned lorry which was balanced on a knife-edge, and could topple over on to them at any moment. Luke bade her curtly,

'Stay out of this. I'll go in on my own.'

But when, a few moments later, he turned instinctively for the help that only she was able to give him, Marion was beside him, and when their patient was finally winched to safety from the tangled metal and sent on his way to hospital and full recovery a few weeks later, Luke raised a thumb to her, and grinned, before growling, 'I told you to stay outside. Now get out, before the thing collapses on us both.'

Marion's heart leapt at the unexpected acknowledgement and her eyes sparked a joyous green signal back, but the gesture of friendliness was not repeated, and once they were back in the Range Rover and heading back towards the hospital, Luke treated her with the same aloof reserve that he had always done, and she supposed wearily that she ought to be thankful that he did not carpet her for indiscipline.

Sometimes they won, and Marion exulted, and sometimes they lost, and she knew that Bill the driver shared her resulting depression. Did Luke share it too, she wondered?

Bill assured her, 'Luke must feel just as shattered as we do. He's human, the same as us. He just doesn't show his feelings, that's all.'

Was Luke human? Marion doubted it. Except for that one isolated occasion, she had never seen him show the slightest reaction one way or the other, and she saw no reason to alter her own diagnosis of him as hard all through.

She stole a glance at his face now, as Bill slowed the Range Rover in response to a signalling police patrol. Except for a narrowing of the blue eyes, Luke's expression did not alter as he assessed the twisted metal that had once been a minibus, and was now wrapped round a lamppost in an inextricable embrace.

Marion felt her stomach churn. She heard Bill mutter an oath, and felt like echoing his sentiments as she followed Luke at speed out of the vehicle.

She was beside him as he raised the rear door of the Range Rover and grabbed his case of equipment from its special slot in the back, and with her own case in her hand, and Bill following with his, they hurried to the stricken minibus.

The next two hours passed in a blur of concentrated energy.

A fireman's terse, 'We'll cut a way in for you in a jiffy, Mr Challoner,' was followed by the police-car driver's thumbnail sketch of events.

'They're a bunch of cadets. They were on their way to a display in town. The front nearside tyre burst, and their bus skidded, and rolled over into the lamppost.'

And then there was no more time for explanations as the firemen's cutting equipment sliced through the tangled metal in an incredibly short space of time, though it seemed like a hundred years to Marion, and the first of the casualties was freed for them to attend to.

Luke worked on one after the other with unhurried calm, yet never wasting a single precious second, infinitely gentle as he tended the frightened children and their distraught and badly injured driver.

Marion worked beside him, all personal feelings temporarily suspended in a cool professional detachment as she called on every ounce of her skill to help alleviate the horrific results of the crash. As usual, she and Luke worked in almost complete silence, linked by the mental telepathy that had grown over the weeks until she felt as if she could read his every thought.

His every thought as a medic. But not as a man.

In spite of their close working relationship, his private thoughts and feelings were a closed book to her, and as she watched the last ambulance ferry its fragile burden away to hospital, the inevitable reaction set in, and with it an overwhelming urge to open the pages of that book, and discover what lay inside the hard cover.

Behind that shuttered face, was Luke, too, suffering from the same boomerang effect of fiddle-tight nerves, suddenly released, and reacting in a human, and very unprofessional, desire to burst into tears?

It was clear from the police-car driver's white, set face that he shared her feelings. Case-hardened by years of motorway patrolling, his voice nevertheless shook as he opined grimly, 'That's one team of cadets won't be marching again for a while. The one little lad will be lucky if he ever walks again. His legs...'

He gulped to a stop, and Luke shot him an impatient look.

'It happens,' he said curtly, and provided the last straw that cracked Marion's professional armour.

Her voice was low but vibrant with anger as the policeman walked away to assist his colleague in controlling the growing flood of home-going evening traffic, and she rounded on Luke and accused him, 'It happens. Is that all you can say? It happens. Full stop. Haven't you got an ounce of human feeling in your whole make-up?'

It was an outrageous way for a mere sister to speak to a surgeon, and her boss into the bargain. It was unprofessional, and unheard of, and once she started Marion found she could not stop.

Her warm mother's heart cried out against the sacrifice of young, eager limbs. Robbie wanted to join the school cadets. He had begged her only last night, 'Can't I, Mum? When I'm big enough? They wear porridge caps.'

Marion laughed, and ruffled the shiny auburn curls that were a mirror image of her own, and promised, 'When you're big enough. And they wear forage caps, not porridge caps.'

The small, warm memory completed what Luke's curt remark had begun.

'Don't you ever see your patients as human beings?' she blazed. 'Or are they simply cases, to you? Not children with shattered limbs, and uncertain futures because of them, but simply clinical challenges to your own cleverness in piecing them together again.'

The steel in Luke's blue eyes cut across the flood like a knife. They latched on to Marion's tight face, and his voice matched their hardness as he snapped, 'It would be better for the police driver if that *was* how he viewed the crash victims. For the sake of his own sanity, and for the sake of the people he is trying to help. If he can't remain detached, he'll be no good at his job. Emotion

is a handicap. If you allow yourself to become personally involved, it spells disaster both for you and the
patient. I would have thought, with your experience, you
would have learned that by now, Sister Rowley.'

Sister Rowley. Not Marion.

It was like a slap in the face, and effectively jerked
Marion's tirade to a halt. It was a deliberate and de-
moralising snub, reminding her that she was a member
of Luke's team only on sufferance.

Emotion is a handicap.

So was being a woman, Marion told herself bitterly.
Luke still made no secret of the fact that he wanted a
man in her place. Someone who was not likely to become
pregnant at an inconvenient moment. And who, his
cutting glance added now, would not be given to un-
seemly emotional outbursts either.

The scorching look welded the gap in Marion's armour
as effectively as his words had opened it, but not before
she had time to feel its searing heat and wince at the
pain of the burn.

Sister Rowley...

Had she only imagined the recent easing of the atmosphere between them since the day of the lorry crash? She
had not realised until now just what that brief moment
of acceptance had meant to her.

Now, she was back where she had started, outside in
the cold, and tolerated only until Luke was able to get
what he regarded as a suitable replacement.

In the strained silence that accompanied their return
journey to the hospital it dawned upon Marion that Luke
had made no attempt to answer her question.

Had he, himself, got any human feelings?

She still did not have the slightest inkling of what he,
personally, felt about the players in the dramas in which
he took so dominant a part. He had slammed shut the

covers of the book before she had gained even a peep at the writing on the pages inside.

'He's impossible,' she fumed to Joy in Casualty later. 'He insists upon treating me as second-best, in spite of my qualifications, and he never loses a single opportunity of putting me down. Anyone would think he paid my salary.'

'He does,' Joy staggered her by saying, and went on to explain, as Marion stared at her, too surprised to comment, 'When the hospital board quibbled over the cost of putting the Flying Squad on the road, he drove a hard bargain. Most people would have appealed for public funds to help. He could have done. He had the local newspapers behind him. But not Mr Challoner.' There was undisguised admiration in her voice. 'He made the fight a personal one. Him against the whole board.'

'He would,' Marion ejaculated with feeling, but Joy ignored the interruption and went on,

'He offered his own services free to the hospital, to fund the Flying Squad for the whole of the year's trial period on which the board insisted.'

'*Free?*' Marion's eyes rounded. 'But, his fees here must amount to...'

'Think of a number, and double it,' Joy grinned. 'The board couldn't refuse his offer, and he knew it. Enter the Flying Squad,' she gestured dramatically.

'He must be mad, or very rich, to be able to make such a crazy bargain.'

'A bit of both,' Joy offered drily. 'But it's the sort of madness I go along with. The Flying Squad has already saved a lot of lives. Mr Challoner's well able to afford his gesture, of course. His people are the upmarket jewellers. You've probably seen their shop in the city. They've got one in most of the major cities here, and on the Continent.'

Marion nodded, slowly absorbing the information. She had wondered why Luke's surname had sounded familiar to her. She had seen the shop in the city often enough. It was the kind of establishment where she only browsed in the window. The price tickets on the discreetly displayed gems denied her entry into the scented portals beyond.

Joy cut across her reflections with, 'His mother is a van Zelt, the Amsterdam diamond-merchant family. That said, he needn't have spent his own money in order to benefit the hospital.'

Perhaps Luke spent it simply in order to get his own way, Marion reflected uncharitably, as she finished cleaning and replenishing the vital equipment boxes from the Casualty department stores, and handed them over to Bill to put back in the Range Rover.

Afterwards she made her way to Luke's office to give him a detailed list of the equipment she had drawn for the purpose. He kept a meticulous account of every tiny item they used, down to each drop of petrol and oil for the vehicle, so that at the end of the trial year he would have hard, unassailable facts to arm him in his final confrontation with the board.

Since her own confrontation with Luke at the scene of the accident, Marion felt a spasm of nerves assail her as she raised her hand to knock on the door of his office.

His curt, 'Come,' was as forbidding as the unyielding wood. Marion despised herself for her accelerated heartbeat as she turned the knob in obedience to the summons, and entered the room. She was not a first-year student, to be browbeaten by a senior consultant. Whether Luke liked it or not, she was a member of the Flying Squad team, and had an equal right to be treated with the respect due to her status.

And she could not help wondering edgily how Luke would address her when they met again.

Would 'Sister Rowley' be the order of the day from now on, except when they were actually out on a call together? Even although she was aware that it contained no personal friendliness, the fact that Luke continued to use her first name in the hospital itself, as well as when they were out on a call, had been a tacit acceptance of her on the team, if only a temporary one.

So, how would he address her now?

In spite of her determination not to show any feeling in front of Luke again, Marion was unable to disguise her apprehension completely, and her eyes flew to the man who sat behind the broad expanse of leather-topped desk facing the door, doubtless writing his report on the incident which they had just attended.

He continued to write for what seemed to Marion endless minutes after she stopped in front of the desk, and he carefully dotted an 'i' and crossed a 't' before he finally glanced up and acknowledged her presence.

Waiting for that acknowledgement, Marion fumed. The man was arrogant. Impossible. Her frown rested on the dark, bent head in front of her, at leisure for the moment to observe while herself being unobserved.

Luke had showered away the road grime that was an inevitable accompaniment to such calls, and had put on a clean uniform, and the dark hair rose in spiky dampness from his high forehead.

The sight of it made Marion's heart do an unexpected somersault. It made Luke, for the first time since she had known him, look oddly vulnerable. Like Robbie, when he was ready for bed, freshly tubbed, and with his hair still clinging damply about his small head.

Marion's hands knew a sudden urge to run her fingers through the dark, damp hair, just as she did with Robbie's. No, not as she did with Robbie's. This urge was an altogether different feeling. An utterly irrational and totally elemental feeling, that shocked her fingers into sudden tight fists to resist the unwelcome intrusion.

The movement creased the neatly written list in her hand, and caused the paper to crackle, and the sound, slight though it was, brought Luke's eyes up to rake her face.

'I've brought my stores list,' she forced out when he did not speak.

'Thank you.'

Not Sister Rowley. Not Marion. Not anything.

Was this how it was to be from now on, until she was replaced by the man he wanted? Bleakness invaded Marion, and she thrust it down, and stood her ground, and listened with outward calm as Luke said, 'I'll attach it to my report.'

He straightened out the creases in the paper caused by her convulsive fingers, his own movements deliberate, his narrowed eyes mocking, if he guessed the cause of those creases, and derided her for each one.

'Incidentally...' Luke rose from his chair with a lithe, easy grace that reminded Marion of the lazy grace of a panther, and he exuded the same threat as he rounded the desk, and his lean height loomed over her.

Involuntarily Marion caught her breath, and his words cut across its slight hiss as he drawled, 'Incidentally, you may feel happier if you know that I haven't included any mention of your—er—outburst in my report. I assume it was a one-off occurrence and won't happen again.'

The threat surfaced, and Marion's breath expelled itself slowly, like air escaping from a pricked balloon. Luke was obliquely accusing her of lack of self-control, an indefensible thing in a nursing sister, that would make her unsuitable for any post of responsibility, not just this one.

Marion's mind froze.

For Robbie's sake she could not—must not—lose this job. In spite of Luke, she had to carry on.

The self-reliance she had learned during the last few years came to her aid, and she faced this new battle head-on, just as she had faced all the others before, and her straightened shoulders and upward-tilted chin were flags of her determination to win through this time as well.

She answered, and her voice crackled ice, ruthlessly kept under control as she forced herself to respond coolly, while she thrust down an almost irresistible longing to pick up the large, oblong blotting-pad that lay on Luke's desk and bring it down upon its owner's arrogant head, to see if that would force some human reaction from him.

He spoke as if she had had an uncontrollable outburst of hysterics at the scene of the accident, which was totally untrue, and he knew it and she knew it, just as she knew vexedly that by letting her guard slip for even a fraction of a minute she had given him one more opportunity to criticise her suitability as a member of his team.

Silently, she vowed, I'll never give him another chance, while out loud she said stiffly, 'Just because we're in the medical profession it doesn't mean that we have to stifle all human feelings towards our patients, particularly when those patients are young children. A little humanity goes a long way to help healing.'

She echoed her own tutor's words, and saw Luke's eyes flicker, but before he could speak she hurried on, 'They weren't youths out joy-riding, as you thought. They were young children, and all of them terribly injured through no fault of their own, and anyone who saw them could not help but feel for them. If they had any heart, that is.'

Had Luke got a heart?

Her own earlier and still unanswered question hung like a challenge in the air between them.

To her disconcertment, he grasped the gauntlet, and his voice was a soft purr as he said, 'You wonder if I've got a heart. Is that it, Marion?'

A menacing purr, that sent his arms with deceptive strength to enclose her in a grip from which there was no escape, as his lips implanted his anger upon her shrinking mouth, punishing her for daring to question him.

Marion reeled under the implacable pressure of his kiss, even as the realisation tracked across her stunned mind. He had called her Marion...

His kiss swept away her defiance and laid siege to her senses, and, stunned into immobility by the sheer un-expectedness of his action, Marion felt her body begin to go pliant in his arms.

This was madness. A wild, wanton madness, such as she had not experienced for many years, and thought she never would again. Luke's lips peeled away the years, and sent fire coursing through her veins, while her mind seemed turned to ice.

For long years she had been a mother, and a nurse, and her own sweet, secret womanhood had lain buried, deep inside her, frozen into a small corner of her heart that feared to let it melt, in case it brought back the agony and the longing that threatened her will to go on.

Since her husband had been killed, Marion had not looked at another man. And now, in one single, dev-astating second, she discovered that her feelings had not died with him as she supposed.

They had only lain dormant, and Luke's kiss awakened them to startled life, and she responded instinctively, as would any attractive woman being kissed by an extra-ordinarily attractive man.

Marion's pulses raced, beating a tattoo of warning in her ears, and a tiny moan escaped her lips that were parted under the pressure of his kiss.

Why, if she had to awaken to life again, did that awakening come at the hands of Luke Challoner, a man whom she heartily detested?

Marion began to struggle in his arms.

Blind fear gripped her, fear of she knew not what. She forgot where she was, who Luke was, and pummelled with ineffectual fists against his chest, striving to beat herself free from the trap of his embrace.

For long minutes he held her fast, moulding her against his hard length, mocking her struggles. And then he released her, so suddenly that she staggered back, and his voice turned from a purr to a snarl as he demanded, 'Does that answer your question, Marion? *Does it?*'

CHAPTER TWO

'DOES that answer your question, Marion? *Does it?*'

It was an answer, and no answer at all, and it posed a dozen more unanswerable questions of its own.

Marion wrenched herself free from Luke's hold and stumbled to the door, and his mocking laugh followed her as she slammed it behind her and lost herself in the blessed sanctuary of the crowded Casualty department.

She trembled all over. Bandages that normally obeyed her expert fingers tumbled across the floor from hands that shook, and the third time it happened Joy gave her a keen look and advised drily, 'Go and give yourself a break. You've been driving yourself like a machine since first light. What's rattling you? Luke Challoner?'

Marion allowed a grimace to answer for her. She felt beyond speech. Rattled was a fair description of how she felt, like a die that had been rudely shaken this way and that until she did not know which number would come out on top.

The prescribed cup of tea steadied her, and she left one in the pot for Joy and emerged to continue her work a few minutes later, outwardly calm, her professional armour restored to hide the torrent that churned inside her and threatened to wash her away on a tide of re-awakened emotions.

'Does that answer your question, Marion?'

Long hours later, Luke's imperious voice pursued her, his words tracking backwards and forwards across her mind with relentless persistence after she put Robbie to bed, and it remained to torment her during the restless hours of the night, demanding with even greater insistence, *'Does it?'*

Marion shrank from trying to find an answer. Her lips still tingled from the pressure of Luke's kiss, her neat waist likewise where his hands had gripped her and moulded her against him, the first pair of male arms to encompass her, except for Robbie's young bear hugs, for six long years.

A brisk soapy shower failed to erase the telltale reminders of Luke's caress, and in a burst of angry impatience Marion tugged the tumbled bedclothes straight for the umpteenth time, and demanded out loud to the darkness, 'Why did it have to be Luke? *Why?'*

Reawakened senses hurt, bringing back the old, aching hunger inside her that no food could assuage, and that she had thought at last she had managed to overcome, and she hated Luke for being the cause of the pain and bewilderment that brought it all back again and scattered her normally carefully schooled emotions into disarray.

The next week started badly.

The Range Rover collected a punctured tyre which added to their running costs on an already tight budget, and a thin drizzle began to fall after a long, dry spell, which turned the traffic-oiled cobblestones in the old part of the town into a veritable skid-pan, and loaded the already overworked Casualty department with a spate of broken wrists and collarbones.

The rain increased in volume to a steady downpour, but in spite of the wet—or because of it? Marion wondered vexedly—Luke called out his crew on even more frequent practice sessions than before, and after the third, totally unnecessary soaking, Marion lost all patience.

'That's the second uniform I've had to change today,' she accused him. 'Can't you at least wait until the worst of the downpour is over before you press that buzzer?'

The sound of the alarm call became an audible goad, probing her raw nerves with the accuracy of a dentist's drill, and she longed to strike away the hand that pressed the signal, but Luke remained unperturbed. He shrugged.

'You've got another uniform. You have to get used to working in rain as well as sunshine. We're not a fair-weather outfit.'

Fair weather was quite the reverse description of her relationship with Luke, Marion thought ruefully. A brewing electric storm would more aptly describe the highly charged atmosphere between them, which erupted into crackling sparks with increasing frequency, that seemed to fly mostly in her direction and burned with a stinging ferocity.

Luke's demands became insatiable, and he was impossible to please, until even the patient Bill was heard to grumble, 'He must be sickening for something. The sooner the spots surface and we can have a bit of peace again, the better.'

It was still raining when they were called out on their first genuine emergency of that week.

Marion felt an almost personal loathing of the rain. It seemed to be waging a vendetta against her. As well as the task of having to launder extra uniforms after their soaking practice sessions, last night Robbie had arrived home from school with muddy clothes and a bleeding kneecap, after having fallen flat into a puddle, which added to the load of washing and ironing which Marion felt wearily she could well do without after her hectic day at the hospital.

Resignedly she tubbed her small son clean, and put a plaster dressing over the graze to protect it. To reward him for not making a fuss she stuck a tiny transfer of

Donald Duck in one corner of the plaster, that was still there when he went to school that morning.

Wheeep! Wheeep! Wheeeeep!

Marion groaned. Another practice session, or a real emergency this time?

The signal was the same for both, and her uprush of resentment against Luke for pressing the buzzer evaporated as the flashing light and blaring siren of the Range Rover warned her that this was a genuine call-out.

Desperation lent her feet wings to speed her to the vehicle ahead of Luke, so that he should not give her the by now accustomed boost up into the high vehicle. Since he had kissed her, she shrank from the prospect of him touching her again, and except for a couple of occasions when she was not quite quick enough, she had managed to avoid any further physical contact with him.

Those two occasions had been enough to warn her of the danger of repeating the experience.

'I ought to have more sense than to let him get under my skin,' Marion scolded herself, but to no avail. The long dormant womanhood in her, which Luke had aroused, refused to be packed back into ice again, and her essentially feminine response to Luke's virile attraction was as unwelcome as it was untimely.

Bill, the driver, was unattached too, and good-looking in a rugged kind of way, so why did not her sensitive nerves react to him in the same pulse-quickening manner? Instead, their antennae swung towards Luke like a compass needle drawn by a magnetic force, and Marion consoled herself with the thought that it was merely physical attraction, and nothing else, and that her wholehearted dislike of the man was the perfect antidote to such unwelcome feelings.

The antidote did nothing to lessen her acute awareness of him as Bill swung the Range Rover out of the hospital gates, and Marion braced her feet on the floor to prevent herself from being swung against Luke, and by dint of muscle-cracking exertion she managed to remain detached as the vehicle straightened and headed through the town.

Smoothing into disciplined routine, Luke leaned forward and flicked the radio switch, and asked the operator at the hospital in that deep, calm, controlled voice that during the past hectic weeks had become the background rhythm of all Marion's days, 'Have you got any details? Give me the gen.'

The operator's disembodied voice answered unemotionally, 'A container lorry ran out of control down Hill Street. It's gone through the school railings at the bottom. Only one casualty reported so far.'

Gone through the school railings...

Cold dread clutched at Marion's heart. Without thinking she glanced at her watch. Three o'clock. Home time for the infant class. Vaguely she was aware of Luke's quick sideways glance, raking her face. Unaware of her own suddenly chalk-white cheeks and ashen lips, and wide eyes filled with a nameless horror.

Only aware of her own heart crying out in anguished pleading, Please, don't let it be Robbie. Not Robbie, too. I can't bear it a second time...

The lorry was still upright. The buckled iron railings had checked its mad career downhill just feet away from the school door. An ambulance man was busy tending the shocked but otherwise uninjured driver, and as the crew ejected from the Range Rover, Marion heard the man's high-pitched voice repeating over and over again, in a nightmare chant, 'The brakes packed up. I couldn't stop it skidding. There was only this one little kid in the school playground. I yelled at him to get out of the way, but he didn't hear me. He was chasing after his balloon.'

The balloon bobbed gently in the breeze against the iron railings, large and red and round, its string caught round the buckled metal, its cheery brightness matching the spreading stain on the grey school sock on its small owner's leg, that lay half hidden by the lorry's front wheel.

Even before Marion's shrinking gaze confirmed her intuition, she knew that, above the rolled-down top of the sock, there would be a piece of adhesive plaster, with a tiny transfer of Donald Duck stuck in the one corner.

Robbie! Oh, Robbie...

No sound came from her bloodless lips, only a gasp as her tightly held breath expelled in a shuddering sigh. A wave of faintness passed over her, and through the swimming scenery Luke's voice reached her, harsh and astringent.

'If you can't stand the sight of injured children, get back in the Range Rover out of the way, and leave this to me.'

Anger, and searing contempt, turned his words into a lash, and they stung Marion back to life again. Luke needed her, and Robbie needed her, and why did she think Luke first, and Robbie second?

There was no time to answer her own question, there was too much to do. With a monstrous effort of will, Marion grasped at the strength of her professional discipline, because her own deserted her at the sight of the small, still face lying on the ground, eyes closed and unresponsive as Luke gently began the task of searching out the extent of the child's injuries.

Contrary to his usual practice, the surgeon spoke. 'He's alive.'

Did he speak to reasure Marion? Or were the words merely an unconscious echo from a heart that existed after all beneath the rock-hard exterior?

Whatever prompted them, they acted like a breath of life to Marion. They brought back her strength, and enabled her hands to respond with their usual sensitivity to Luke's every requirement as he began the task of preparing his injured patient for the journey to hospital, and only the extra brilliance of Marion's green eyes betrayed her anguish as she worked through the nightmare that haunts the dreams of every medic, that of battling for the life of someone they personally love.

At last it was over. The ambulance men lifted the stretcher with its small burden and slid it into the ambulance, and Luke briefly warned the hospital on the Range Rover's wireless, 'No head injuries. Spine seems to be OK. One hip gone. Might be internal injuries, I can't be sure. I'll travel back in the ambulance with him.'

'Let me come, too.' The words were wrung out of Marion.

Luke's cold glance cut them short, and he refused her curtly. 'There isn't room. We're taking the lorry driver with us as well, he's badly shocked. Clear up here, and return in the Range Rover with Bill.'

Without waiting for more, he was gone, and the ambulance doors closed behind him, and the vehicle drew away, taking with it everything that made life worth living for Marion.

Mechanically she cleared away. She even found time to reassure Sue, who had come to the school to collect Robbie and the twins as usual, displaying a brittle confidence that did absolutely nothing to reassure herself.

'I'll drop in when I come off duty, and let you know how Robbie is,' she promised her next-door neighbour, and only when she was back in the privacy of the Range Rover with Bill, in the cab that seemed strangely, bleakly empty without Luke, did she begin to shake.

Bill was kind. He comforted, 'We'll all be off duty by the time we get back to base, so Luke will be free to operate on Robbie himself. The little lad couldn't be in better hands.'

Marion knew that. Just as she knew that Bill's kindness made things worse. She needed the type of strength that only Luke seemed able to give her, the iron discipline which she had railed against but which kept her on her feet and working at maximum efficiency long after most people would have given up.

His was an abrasive strength, that complemented the endurance she had learned during the last difficult years, that had served the same purpose until Luke's kiss had released the essential feminine weakness that she had so ruthlessly locked away when her husband died, and which now eroded that strength just when she needed it most.

Writing her report with far from steady hands, Marion condemned Luke for what he had done to her, made worse by the nightshift crew offering with mistaken kindness, when Bill explained the identity of their latest patient, 'We'll top up the emergency boxes for you. You write your report, and then go and see how your little boy is getting on.'

Which left Marion with very little to do, and time on her hands that for once she was unable to fill. Joy had gone off duty, and the time of day was that no-man's-land between the morning re-dressings and rush-hour casualties and the evening crowd of damaged revellers, that left the staff with their only breathing-space of the day, and for once no need of Marion's offer to help them.

She sat with nail-biting impatience, willing the time to pass, numbly receiving from the staff the tea and sympathy she so often extended to waiting relatives herself.

A lifetime passed before the night sister in charge of Casualty came to her and said, 'Robbie's been warded, and he's beginning to come round. It's all right for you to go up and see him now.'

Marion took the stairs two at a time. In an explosion of pent-up nerves she could not bear to wait for the lift, and she reached the door of the second-floor ward flushed and out of breath. Robbie was in a small side room off the main ward, reserved for post-op recovery cases, and the ward sister greeted her with unconcealed surprise.

'Hello, Marion. They said the little boy's mother was waiting downstairs, but I'd no idea it was you.'

'How...?' Marion's eyes beseeched her.

'Not as bad as it looked,' the other woman hastened to reassure her. 'He's got a broken femur, but there aren't any internal injuries, thank goodness, and it's a clean break. He'll be as good as new, and up to all sorts of mischief again just as soon as it's mended.'

'Thank God.' Marion's eyes suddenly swam, releasing the unbearable tension that stretched her nerves to breaking-point and beyond, and she was hardly aware of the sister's kindly,

'Go in now and take a look for yourself. You can stay with him for a while, although he's very drowsy and he will soon drop off again. You look as if you could do with a rest yourself.'

'I can cope.'

Marion felt that she could cope with anything, even Luke, now that Robbie was going to be all right. Nevertheless, it came as a shock to see Luke sitting beside the cot when she entered the ward. She had not expected to find the surgeon still with his small patient, and from the scowl that crossed Luke's face as she came through the door and he looked round and saw her, the surprise was mutually disagreeable.

He scowled, and although he kept his voice low in deference to his patient, there was no mistaking his anger as he growled, 'I warned you before not to get personally involved with your patients. How many times...?'

'I *am* personally involved with this patient, whether you like it or not,' Marion retorted clearly, and stepped up to the side of the cot.

The guard rail was still down on the nearest side, and at the sound of Marion's voice its occupant turned his head and opened drowsy eyes and looked up at her and mumbled, 'Mommy?'

That small word was nearly Marion's undoing. For a second or two her face worked, and she had to fight hard to retain her self-control. Since gaining the coveted status of full-time schoolboy, Robbie had steadfastly turned his back on infantile things, and except in times of crisis such as when he tumbled over, he now insisted upon calling his mother by what he considered to be the more grown-up title of Mum.

The little boy complained sleepily, 'I lost my balloon. Adam was going to swap it for his conker. It's a one-er.'

So that was why Robbie had been chasing after his balloon, so intent upon its recovery that he did not hear the lorry driver shout at him. A vision of the scarlet sphere bobbing above the twisted iron railings of the school playground closed Marion's eyes for a brief, agonised second.

All for the want of a horseshoe nail... Only this had been a balloon. And a conker. A one-er, whatever that meant. She swallowed hard, and managed, 'Maybe if I ask Adam nicely, he'll let me have the conker for you after all. I can buy him another balloon to swap.'

'Will you, Mommy? Promise? He'll be... at the... bonfire...'

The words tailed off, and Robbie's eyelids drooped, and on Marion's quiet assurance, 'I promise,' the night sister appeared and ordered her in a firm aside,

'Off you go now, and get some rest yourself. You look all in. He'll sleep the clock round, and you would benefit by doing the same.'

Marion cast a longing look at the face of her now quietly sleeping son. Her warm mother's heart yearned to remain with Robbie, to wait and watch beside him in case he should wake up and want her.

Her professional experience told her that he would not, and that the ward sister's advice was sound. She herself had echoed it many times to anxious relatives, and now knew the amount of strength it took to bend and kiss the little sleeping face, and obediently turn away.

She smiled mechanically at the ward sister and blinked her eyes clear to locate the ward door, and felt a familiar firm grip close round her elbow, and steer her unerringly in the right direction.

Luke seemed to have a propensity for propelling her through doorways. A shaky urge to giggle assailed Marion, and was choked off by the hard painful lump in her throat that denied her the ability to protest as he hurried her along beside him, taking in the seemingly endless corridor and the stairs in grim-faced silence.

When they came opposite to the door to his office, he reached out his free hand and wrenched at the handle, and before Marion was aware of what he was about to do, he swung through the opening with herself in tow.

'I've already put my report on your desk,' she protested. 'I'm off duty now.'

'So am I, so we can cut out the formalities,' he rasped back. 'I'm not interested in your written report of the accident right now. It's a personal report, from you, that I want.' Both his hands gripped her now, one on either arm, resisting her convulsive move to break away from him, and he turned her back and held her firmly facing him. 'Why didn't you tell me, Marion?' he demanded roughly.

'Tell you what? I don't know what you mean.'

'Don't stall. You know full well what I mean. Why didn't you tell me while we were at the school that the patient was your own child? *Why*, Marion?'

'You didn't give me the chance.'

The long, exacting day on duty, adding to the mental toll of the last few hours since finding Robbie under the lorry, loosened Marion's tongue, and she told him why, without any reservations. If he wanted to cut out the formalities of a boss-cum-member-of-staff relationship, that was fine by her, and hang the consequences. Marion felt too drained to care as she accused Luke bitterly, 'If I'd tried to tell you, you wouldn't have listened.'

'You could have tried me. You went so white, I thought...'

'You thought the worst of me, as usual. You misread the evidence, and acted as judge, jury and executioner. Doesn't it ever occur to you that there might be another answer than the figure you arrive at when you've done your sums? Two and two *don't* always make five.'

Marion should have felt better for her outburst. According to all medical lore, letting off steam helped to clear the air, and brought a sense of relief.

In her case, it had exactly the opposite effect. A deep blanket of depression descended upon her, and she blamed it on the stress of the day, and valiantly she tried to fight free from it. She found herself instead fighting against the increasing pressure of Luke's arms that drew her closer and closer against him.

'Do I seem such an ogre to you?' he asked. 'Do you still believe that I haven't got a heart? Perhaps this will convince you.'

His hands released her arms, and caught her fingers instead, and pressed them palm-flat against his broad chest, forcing them to remain there and register the strong, steady beat of the organ whose very existence Marion questioned.

Only a thin silk shirt and a starched white hospital coat separated her hands from his chest, and they did nothing to muffle the regular rhythm underneath as it pulsed its message through her finger-ends.

The feel of it sent a wave of sensation coursing through Marion. It was as if she was tuning in to the essential, dynamic life-force of this enigmatic man, touching on elemental secrets of his closely guarded, private world, that she might be able to read if only she could break the code of that rhythmic beat, pulsing its stirring message through the thin covering of cloth.

As well as driving the blood through Luke's veins, it seemed to be pumping it at increasing speed through her own as well, taking over the task from her own heart, which began to palpitate in a breath-destroying manner that, Marion assured herself without conviction, must be reaction from having just been to see Robbie.

Her pulses jerked unevenly, causing her colour to come and go. She longed to use her hand to cover the hot tide of confusion which made her cheeks rival her curls for brilliance, and condemned the delicate skin that went with her lovely hair for betraying her feelings to the brilliant blue gaze that riveted on her face.

She tried to snatch her hands away, but strong surgeon's fingers clamped them tight. She tried to twist away from him, but Luke's one arm went round her waist, moulding her against him and preventing any movement.

In desperation, Marion used the only other armour left to her, and dropped her lashes against the piercing brilliance of those blue eyes that strove to read her very thoughts.

Luke released her hands then, and used his own freed fingers to tip up her chin, so that she was forced to look up again and meet that mesmerising stare, as he re-

peated the question that his own action had just
answered.

'Does that convince you?'

Whatever answer Marion might have given was lost
as Luke's lips took away her power of speech.

The last time there had been anger in his kiss that had
roused a saving anger in Marion to ward off the vital
male charisma of this man, but this time his lips withheld
that antidote, and stroked instead across her own with
a disarming gentleness, their pressure a sensual seeking
that penetrated Marion's hastily erected defences, and
roused a wild disturbance in her, compounded of a mix
of fear and excitement that set her every nerve tingling.

Luke's kiss convinced her, and made her wish that she
had never asked the question in the first place, but it
was too late now, and she hastily thrust aside another
question which presented itself unasked to her bemused
mind.

Too late for what?

At last, Luke let her go. He raised his head, and his
arms dropped to his sides, but Marion still stood transfixed, her eyes wide green pools of dismay as she stared
up into his face.

'Cat's eyes,' he mocked, and bent again and lightly
kissed their lids, making them blink. The movement
broke the spell, and Marion jinked away from him, and
a taunting smile crooked his lips, but all he said was,
'Time to go.'

He hitched his white coat on to the stand and shrugged
into his suit jacket, and taking her by the elbow again—
did he think she was incapable of walking on her own?—
he steered her once more through the doors, only this
time Marion felt no urge to giggle at the repetition.

The cool air outside restored her poise somewhat, and
when Luke asked, 'Where is your car parked?' she
gathered enough presence of mind to hedge.

'It's ... er ...'

She allowed her voice to trail away, and began to fumble in her shoulder-bag as if she was searching for ignition keys, while she wondered desperately, Why doesn't he go away and leave me alone? Why did he not get into his own car, the sleek, low-slung, mist-grey Jaguar, parked in the slot reserved for consultants on the other side of the car park, and drive away, and remain in ignorance of her implied lie that must reveal itself when she made her way to the bus stop?

The seconds began to stretch, and Marion thought frantically, I can't go on searching for non-existent keys for ever, when the swing doors from Casualty opened behind her and one of the night-duty staff came through. Seeing her he sang out cheerily, 'You've just missed the number ten, Marion. I saw it leave the bus stop about five minutes ago.'

He strode on his way whistling, and Marion glared at his retreating figure. Why did the man have to choose now, of all times, to tell her that she had missed her bus? Her fumbling fingers froze into immobility, and she felt Luke stiffen beside her.

'Why didn't you tell me you had to wait for a bus?'

Marion's hackles rose at his peremptory tone. It was no business of his if she travelled by bicycle or Rolls-Royce. She opened her mouth to tell him so, but before the words could emerge, Luke demanded, 'How long is it before the next one is due?'

'Not long.'

He gave an exclamation of impatience. 'It's like trying to prise open a clam to get any information out of you. *How long?* I said.'

The returning night-staff member answered for her. 'Every half-hour or so. That is, if they run on time, which they don't very often.' He vanished back through the swing doors, sublimely unaware of the silent maledictions which Marion sent in his wake.

Luke said abruptly, 'I'll take you home.'

'There's no need. There's nearly fifteen minutes of the half-hour gone already. It won't be long before...'

'...so get into the car, and don't argue. We'll be there long before the bus.'

Luxurious comfort enveloped Marion as she sank into the deep passenger seat, and Luke shut the door on her with a well-upholstered thud that seemed an echo of his own determination to get his own way. He was silent as he drove through the evening traffic, and Marion made no attempt to break it.

She had more than enough to occupy her mind without the added strain of parrying any more remarks from Luke. The wide sweep of the windscreen wipers, dealing with yet another shower, swung in a mesmeric arc in front of her, like a metronome beating out the rhythm of her disturbed thoughts.

One kiss, two kiss, three kiss, four...

One kiss from Luke was one too many, so far as she was concerned. It roused feelings she did not want to resurrect, that had no place in their professional relationship. The second kiss left her shaken to the core, and warned of potential disaster if it should be repeated.

Bitterly Marion resented Luke kissing her. Earlier she had resented his aloofness, but that was different. She could handle that, and herself, while he remained distant from her.

Handling Luke at closer quarters, and the feelings he seemed capable of arousing in her with such humiliating ease, was an altogether different matter, and Marion's confidence wavered.

She cast a longing look at the bus rumbling in front of them, the one she had just missed, and began urgently, 'If you drop me off at the next...'

Luke ignored her, accelerated round the vehicle, and passed the next bus stop as if it did not exist, and the closer they got to her home, the tighter Marion's nerves became, until she wanted to scream at Luke to stop the car, and allow her to get out and walk the rest of the way alone, if only to seek escape in physical exercise from the fog of mental confusion that rivalled the driving rain in its bid to cloud her normally clear inner vision.

Contrarily, she dreaded going into the house on her own. The coming experience threatened to repeat that other dreadful time when she had first been obliged to enter an empty house, and face a future as bleak as its silent rooms.

She glanced at the illuminated dial of the clock on the dashboard. It was later than she thought. By now Sue would be putting the twins to bed and preparing her husband's evening meal, and it would be unfair to interrupt her routine, so there was no escape in that direction.

Immersed in her own thoughts, Marion started when Luke spoke.

'Is your house number five, or number fifteen?'

She roused and looked about her, and saw they were already entering her own street. Luke had not asked her where she lived, so...

'How did you know?'

'I remember the address from your application form.'

That was months ago now. The man must have a phenomenal memory, even if he could not recall the exact house number. Marion confessed grudgingly, 'Number fifteen,' and knew with a feeling of inevitability that Sue would be agog behind her curtains as the big car drew up smoothly outside her own modest semi.

A stranglehold of pain gripped her throat as Luke rounded the car to help her to alight. When she arrived home late, Robbie always raced from next door to greet her. Luke sent a comprehensive glance to her set face, and said, 'Give me your key.'

He did not wait for her to argue. He took it from her hand and fitted it into the lock of the front door, and his height seemed to dwarf the small hall as he followed her inside.

Without thinking, Marion walked straight through and into the kitchen, edgily aware of Luke treading closely on her heels. She was bleakly aware of the emptiness that lay as much inside herself as in the deserted room.

A toy car lay against the sink unit, abandoned in Robbie's last-minute scramble to get ready for school that morning. Automatically Marion bent to pick it up, and turned to put it on the table.

Luke stood watching her. Hastily she compressed her lips in a bid to iron out their betraying tremble. It was Luke's fault that the tremble was there in the first place. If he had not infiltrated the chink in her armour she would have been able to cope better than this, and present her usual briskly cheerful face to the world, whatever she might feel like inside.

Her chin tilted, defying him to read her weakness, and for a second a strange expression stirred in the depths of the blue eyes, and then it was gone, and Luke said casually, 'Give the car to me. I've got to go back and do ward rounds later on tonight. I'll put the toy in Robbie's cot, for him to find as soon as he wakes up in the morning.' He removed the toy from her fingers, and added, 'Now get the cups out, while I put the kettle on.'

Surprise compelled Marion to obey him. She turned towards the cupboard that held the crockery, and heard the tap begin to run behind her. Luke allowed sufficient water out to clear the pipe before he put the kettle underneath to catch a filling, and Marion eyed him wonderingly.

She had never associated Luke with such a homely, mundane task. Other people brought the surgeon tea, and did the washing up afterwards. This time it appeared that he was prepared to help do both. He twisted the lid off the coffee jar, spooned granules into the cups, and reached for the sugar bowl.

'I don't take...' Marion began, and Luke looked up briefly and contradicted,

'You do tonight,' and deliberately stirred a generous spoonful into her cup while omitting it from his own.

'Drink it,' he commanded, and pushed the cup across the table to her.

Marion eyed the dark liquid, and its donor, and quick temper warmed her cheeks. She longed to thrust it back at him and cry, 'Drink it yourself.' But she had tried to defy Luke before with disastrous consequences, and she did not feel capable of engaging in another unequal battle tonight.

Weariness overwhelmed her. The sugar would help, which was why Luke had used it, but that knowledge did nothing to stem her resentment at his dictatorial manner, and she sipped reluctantly, her hands cradling the hot cup, warming them outside as the coffee warmed her within.

It restored her sufficiently to enable her to grimace at the unaccustomed sweetness, so that Luke should know she was drinking it under protest, as a restorative, and not because he told her to.

She said, 'The car will keep Robbie occupied until I can bring him the conker from Adam.'

Talking about Robbie made a bridge between herself and Luke, and thankfully she allowed her feet to lead her along it, fearful of the quagmire of unspoken thoughts and unanswered questions which threatened her from either side.

Their conversation was desultory. Luke seemed content to allow her to take the lead for once, and sipped his own coffee in a brooding silence, responding in monosyllables until Marion ran out of things to say, and she breathed a sigh of relief when the coffee was finished and she could grasp at domesticity as a release from the growing tension between them.

She collected the used cups into the sink and ran water into a bowl, and Luke unhooked the tea towel from the side of the sink unit, and cautioned, 'Get Robbie's father to teach him how to use his conker without hitting his thumb. He's damaged enough for the moment, without inviting more.'

Marion felt that nothing about Luke would surprise her again. He had slipped off his suit jacket and laid it across the back of his chair, and the brightly printed linen glass-cloth, a present from Sue and her family from their last seaside holiday, struck an incongruous note against the immaculate cuffs of his pure silk shirt, but he appeared to be in no way disconcerted, and Marion rallied from the contrast and answered him flatly, 'Robbie's father is dead.'

'Is that what you've told the boy?'

It took several seconds before the meaning of his words hit Marion. She turned towards him, puzzled, with the washing-up brush held in her right hand and a soapy cup in the other. The suds began to drip, and hastily she swilled it under the tap, clearing the bubbles from the utensil and from her hand at the same time.

Luke's eyes followed her movement, and with a sense of shock Marion saw them fix on the third finger of her left hand. The finger from which her wedding ring had been cut and was now too small to go over the damaged knuckle.

Slowly the implication of Luke's words penetrated, and Marion went rigid. It was like being struck by a dart from a blowpipe, spreading its poison through every fibre of her being.

And it had been aimed at her, quite deliberately, by Luke.

Her eyes flashed green fire. Gone was her weariness, and gone, too, was the erstwhile confusion of her thoughts. They crystallised on one thing with a vivid clarity.

She hated Luke Challoner.

'You...you...' she ground out, and her fingers clenched round the hapless cup, threatening the life of the fine bone china that, if it broke, would spoil a precious wedding present.

Her cheeks flew scarlet flags of outrage, and Luke's eyes narrowed to blue slits, gauging the chances that she might hurl the cup at him.

'Cooeee, Marion. It's me. Can I come in?' The letterbox flap rattled, and Sue's voice called through the slit. Marion turned her head, and the would-be missile became a harmless cup again and clattered on to the draining board, and Luke picked it up and began to wipe it dry, and remarked calmly, as if nothing had happened,

'Hadn't you better open the door, before whoever it is wrecks your letterbox?'

'It's Sue. She's my next-door neighbour.'

The words came out jerkily, conventional explanations that fell from her lips while other, unrelated words burned indelibly in her brain.

How dared Luke! How *dared* he?

She opened the front door, and felt vaguely astonished at the outward calm with which she greeted her neighbour, the while she trembled inside as if with an ague.

Logic asked Marion what other interpretation Luke could put on a ringless left hand, and the presence in a hospital cot of her five-year-old son, but she felt beyond logic.

In any situation where she was concerned, Luke invariably thought the worst of her. He added two and two and made five, and then blamed her, Marion, for his own iniquitous arithmetic. Through a daze of anger she heard him answer Sue's anxious questions with, 'Robbie will be as right as rain. It'll take a while for his leg to heal, of course. He'll be immobilised for some time, but he's quite comfortable.'

As comfortable as can be expected... Marion's lips gave a bitter twist. How often had she, herself, used the same meaningless phrase? It was the very last description that could apply to her own feelings now.

Her mind simmered. She felt as if at any moment it might boil over, and above the bubbling cauldron she heard Sue chatter on, 'I shall feel too scared to let the twins go back to school after this, at least until the railings are replaced round the playground. What if another lorry...?'

'I'm sure the headmaster will take adequate precautions,' Luke soothed.

'He'd better. My husband says he's going to have a talk with him when we go to the school bonfire tomorrow evening,' Sue answered grimly, and turned to Marion. 'I suppose you won't be coming with us, now?'

'I must. Robbie made me promise to ask Adam for a conker.'

Normal, everyday conversation, dropping from abnormally stiff lips, while all the while Marion's tongue longed to shout at Luke, 'I hate you. I hate you'.

Her eyes conveyed the message for her when he said, 'I must go. I've still got my ward rounds to do,' and politeness forced her to accompany him to the front door.

She paused with her hand raised, holding the latch, and caught her breath as for a long moment he stood over her, looking down, and reading the green fire that burned fiercely up into his face.

Briefly his own eyes narrowed again, resisting the fire, but in the semi-darkness of the porch his face lay in shadow, and Marion was unable to read his expression. After an endless pause he said, 'Don't stay awake worrying about Robbie. I meant it when I said he's going to be fine.'

And then he was gone. Without another word he pivoted on his heel, his shoes scuffing briefly on the coconut mat of the porch floor, and strode away along the short garden path.

Treading the rough surface under his heel, which was where, arrogantly, he had just trampled her character.

CHAPTER THREE

IN spite of Luke's reassurance, Marion found it difficult to sleep that night.

Her longing to see Robbie drove her to catch the first bus to the hospital the next morning, and she complied willingly when the ward sister co-opted her help.

'Give him his bath and breakfast while you're here, if you've got the time,' she begged. 'We're one short on the night staff, and it's making us late all round.'

'I've got plenty of time. I don't go on duty for another hour.'

Marion gladly concentrated her attention on her small son's needs, finding an outlet for her own pent-up emotions in the process. Robbie was fretful, hating the restriction of having to remain in bed, and mortified at finding himself confined in a cot with pull-up sides.

'I'm not a baby,' he complained, and Marion lied hastily,

'It's only because they're short of proper beds. Make the best of it, there's a lamb.'

It was an all-too-familiar refrain. Robbie had had to make the best of a lot of shortcomings in his five years, Marion thought sadly, and to distract him she turned the subject.

'Tell me which one is Adam, so I'll know who to ask for your conker at the bonfire tonight.'

'He's the one with the tooth missing in the middle. You won't forget, will you, Mum? His conker is a one-er.'

She was back to being called Mum again. Joy flooded through her, even while she wondered.

At a crowded school bonfire party, what was the likelihood of being able to track down one small boy with a tooth missing in the middle?

If she succeeded, what if Adam had changed his mind, and refused to part with his conker after all? With the fickleness of childhood, he might decide to keep his conker for himself. If so, where was she to find another one to replace it, so as not to disappoint Robbie?

A voice cut across her wonderings. 'When you get your conker, ask your mother to show you how to use it without hitting your thumb.'

Luke! Marion's heart missed a beat, and then made up for it by accelerating in the now familiar, disconcerting reaction whenever the surgeon came upon her unawares.

Robbie saved her from having to speak. 'Mum can't play conkers,' he scoffed. 'Girls can't aim straight. She hit her finger once with a hammer, and made it go all funny.'

The third finger on her left hand. Marion's cheeks burned as Luke's eyes dropped to assess the distorted knucklebone.

'So I see,' he replied coolly. 'Next time, you'd do better to leave things to a professional.'

'I can't afford to employ a workman every time I need to knock a nail in something.'

The unspoken reason for her needing to use the tool herself, that of having no man around to do the job for her, loaded the air between them, and returning anger at the memory of last night put an effective brake on Marion's racing pulse. She glanced ostentatiously at her watch, and said to Robbie, 'I must go now, poppet. I'm on duty in a few minutes. I'll come back and see you whenever I can. Be good, won't you?'

Robbie was accustomed to the discipline of his mother being 'on duty' and he accepted it philosophically.

'Come as soon as you can, won't you?' he pleaded. 'Thanks for bringing my car for me.'

'I didn't bring it. Luke did.'

Without thinking, Marion used the surgeon's first name, and knew sudden confusion as her eyes rose to his, and met his derisory stare.

'Er, I mean, Mr Challoner,' she corrected herself hastily.

'Luke will do,' he cut across her apology, and reached for the clipboard that hung on the end of the cot and began to study its graphics. 'How does your leg feel this morning, Robbie?'

It was not quite a snub, but his action made Marion immediately superfluous, dismissing her to the ranks of a visitor, unwanted on ward rounds. The ward sister hovered, a silent reminder that, because Marion was a member of the hospital staff, it did not give her any special privileges. She took the hint.

'See you later.' She gave Robbie a wave, and hurried out to Casualty, where a for once full complement of staff on duty, with no one on holiday or away sick, enabled her to pop up to see Robbie twice more during the morning.

Each time she returned heartened by the little boy's maintained improvement, and for once the buzzer in her pocket remained inexplicably silent. She remarked on the unusual event to Joy.

'Luke must be either uncommonly busy, or suffering from a mental aberration. He hasn't called us out on a single practice session yet today.'

The Casualty Sister gave her a thoughtful look. 'You do have it in for Luke Challoner, don't you? Why? I would have thought you would have got to know him better by now, after working with him all these months.'

Getting to know Luke better was the root cause of the trouble, although not quite in the sense which Joy meant, but Marion had no intention of confiding in her that far, and she answered offhandedly, 'Let's say we're just not compatible,' and left it at that.

When her buzzer continued to remain silent, Marion checked it to make sure that it was working properly. Luke would be sure to lay the blame on her shoulders for whatever reason, if he pressed the emergency buzzer and she failed to answer the call.

The small pocket receiver made its usual instant response to her check, however, and her puzzlement increased.

'Wonders never cease,' she shrugged, but she felt thankful for the unusual reprieve that allowed her, for once, to go off duty at the appointed time, and be with Robbie for long enough to read him the accustomed bedtime story, tuck him up, and promise for the umpteenth time, 'I won't forget to ask Adam for your conker.'

If she hurried, she might just be in time to catch the early bus. It would give her breathing-space when she got home, to grab a quick snack before she joined Sue and her family, who were providing her with transport to the school.

She was crossing the car park to the main gate of the hospital when Luke caught up with her. Marion heaved a sigh of pure exasperation. The bus was due in a couple of minutes. She had not set eyes on Luke since they had met at Robbie's cot early that morning, so what on earth could he want with her now?

Tense with impatience she spun to face him.

He remarked conversationally, 'You must have had a peaceful day, with no call-outs.'

Marion eyed him warily. Was he setting a trap for her? She was certain there had not been any call-outs. If there had been, and her bleeper was not working after all, she knew Luke would have no scruples in leaving her behind, but surely Bill would have sought her out afterwards and warned her of the wrath to come.

The suggestion that he might have refrained out of consideration to herself, in order to allow her time to go and see Robbie at intervals during the day, tracked across her mind, and she dismissed it impatiently. Consideration was not in Luke's make-up. He was hard all through.

She said defensively, 'There weren't any calls. I checked my bleeper, and it was working OK, so...'

'Let me see?'

Luke held out his hand, and with a desperate look in the direction of the bus stop, Marion perforce had to fish out her bleeper from under her cape, and hand it over to him.

'Mmm, yes, it seems fine.'

He took an inordinate time fiddling with the small receiver, and Marion's impatience reached explosion point as her nerve-stretched ears caught the sound of the number ten bus rumbling up the hill towards the hospital stop.

'I'll tuck it back in your pocket for you.'

'I can tuck it back myself. I don't need you to do it for me.'

If she grabbed the receiver, and ran as fast as her feet would carry her, she might just make it to the bus stop in time. Her fingers closed round the receiver, but unexpectedly Luke hung on.

'Don't snatch,' he chided.

'I must fly, or I'll miss...ooooh!'

The last of her breath expelled in a rush of exasperation as the bus approached the stop, and seeing no one waiting there the driver accelerated away again.

'You've missed it,' Luke informed her unnecessarily, and Marion's patience snapped.

'You did that on purpose,' she blazed.

'Which is why I'm going to take you home, or you'll miss the start of the bonfire as well.'

'I could...I could...' Marion choked.

What she felt she could do to Luke at that moment would be better not put into words. He supplied them urbanely. 'You could do with a lift home, so get in.'

Marion's protests were as effective as trying to shelter under a parasol in a monsoon. Luke swept them aside, shrugged off her indignation, and deposited her in the front passenger seat of the Jaguar, and Marion thought bemusedly, as the big car cruised away from the hospital, All this has happened before.

It was like a re-run of a familiar movie, even to Luke taking her door-key from her fingers and opening the front door of her house for her, and after a short pause, in which she heard him speak to Sue over the fence, treading closely on her heels along the hall on the way to the kitchen.

This time there was no toy car on the floor.

Before Marion could react to the lack, Luke remarked, 'I'll put the kettle on while you go upstairs and get changed into whatever ladies consider suitable for going to a bonfire party.'

'I'm going with Sue and her family.'

'I've just told Sue that I'm taking you.'

'*You're* going to the school bonfire? But...you're not a parent, so why?'

It came as a shock to think that he could be, even though she knew that he was not married. Resentment stirred in her afresh. He had condemned her for that very reason. Although he had not said the words out loud, his attitude had spoken for itself.

It was a man's world.

'I'm not a parent.' The quiet statement cut Marion's anger off at root level and, deflated, she stared at him numbly as he went on, 'But I am the broom that has to sweep up the bits, when there's an accident like the one at the school. I want to make sure that it isn't repeated. Like Sue's husband, I, too, want to see the headmaster, and find out what steps are being taken safety-wise. So go and get changed, and be quick about it. I don't want to be late.'

He did not want to be late. His effrontery took Marion's breath away. She sent him a searing look that should have dented his self-assurance, and instead provoked a taunting grin in reply that pursued her as she went on her way upstairs.

She had exchanged her hospital uniform for a cream cowl-necked sweater and a jade-green trouser-suit that deepened the green of her eyes and took a disconcerting ten years from her normally poised twenty-six, when she realised that, because Luke had driven her home, she had not remembered to stop off at the corner shop on the way to buy a scarlet balloon that was to be the necessary exchange for the coveted conker.

'You made me forget to buy a balloon,' she blamed Luke as she ran downstairs.

'I've brought a packet of balloons with me. There's bound to be a red one among them. It was a red one, wasn't it?'

He sorted among the packet until he found one of the desired colour, and Marion said tightly, 'You think of everything, don't you?'

'I've thought of something else, as well,' he said mysteriously, and delved into his pocket again.

He had changed as well, Marion saw. While she had been upstairs, he had shed his car coat against the warmth of the centrally heated kitchen and revealed a beautifully knitted Aran sweater over casual slacks and stoutly soled slip-ons that were a far cry from the neat, hand-made shoes which he wore at the hospital.

'What else?'

'This.' Carefully, almost reverently, he unravelled a short length of string, at the end of which dangled a large, shiny conker. He swung it triumphantly in front of Marion's nose. 'It's a one-er,' he told her gravely.

An irresistible urge to giggle assailed Marion. First the bonfire, and now a conker. Was there no end to the surprises which this impossible man was capable of springing on her?

She burbled helplessly, 'What on earth's a one-er?'

'It's the same as a knock-out in boxing. One smack, and your opponent's conker is shattered. And probably his fingers as well, if he's not careful.'

Luke's eyes twinkled down into hers, the carefree, merry eyes of a boy who loved to play conkers, and who knew the agony of banged fingers, and wanted to save Robbie from suffering in the same way.

A warmth took away Marion's anger at the un-expected thoughtfulness, made warmer still when Luke added, 'Children can be changeable. I thought I'd bring a conker along, just in case Robbie's friend has changed his mind and won't do a swap after all. On top of having a broken bone, it would be a shame to disappoint him about the conker.'

Marion said impulsively, 'I can't imagine you playing conkers.'

'I was conker champion at prep school. And I still get lots of practice with the small fry of the family.'

'Do you belong to a big family?' It was none of her business, but suddenly she felt she wanted to know.

'I've got two brothers and two sisters. They're all married, and I'm awash with nieces and nephews.'

His grin was infectious. It swept away the stern professional exterior which was all Marion had known of him until now, and allowed an unexpected, fun-loving boy to peep through, who invited Marion to climb out of her own professional shell and join him.

Surprise warred with laughter, and laughter won, and swept away the barriers between them. The kettle whistled a warning, and Luke made the tea as if he had done it hundreds of times before, and Marion cut chunks of rich fruit cake, and wondered why her hastily baked offering which was several days old should taste so good.

Could it be because Luke was sitting across the table from her, sharing the simple repast?

The possibility sobered Marion, and she was silent as Luke drove them to the bonfire shortly afterwards. He glanced round at her withdrawn face, but Marion was too immersed in her own thoughts to notice, and Luke did not speak until he drew to a halt in the school play-ground, around which Marion's apprehensive glance told her the railings had already been replaced with a stout crash-barrier.

'It isn't like the Town Council to get things done this quickly,' she exclaimed.

'I leaned on them,' Luke admitted and, reading her startled look, he circumvented her questions by taking her by the arm and commanding, 'Let's go and find Adam, and haggle for his conker. What sort of child are we looking for? Thin? Fat? Freckles?'

'One with a tooth missing in the middle.'

'Sounds geriatric,' Luke quipped, and the laughter was back, and he swung Marion's hand gaily in his as they went in search of their quarry.

They sought help from the teacher of infants.

'Adam?' She shook her head. 'He hasn't come. He went down with a dreadful cold last night, and his mother's had to keep him indoors. I'm so glad Robbie's going to be all right. The children are all busy crayoning get-well cards to send to him.'

Thank goodness for Luke's conker! Marion's expressive face mirrored her thanks, and Luke ducked them with a quick invitation. 'Have a roast potato?'

He selected a potato from a tray offered by a passing teacher, and split it into two between them. It was hot, and covered in ashes from the bonfire, and the outside was cooked and the inside was still raw.

'Rotten chef,' Luke grimaced, and Marion agreed, 'Mmmm,' but she bit into it just the same, and any loss of expertise in the baking was more than made up for by sharing it with Luke.

She knew she was playing with fire, and not of the variety which burned in a flaming cone behind them, but for the moment she ceased to care.

The knowledge that Robbie was recovering well released her mind from the chains of anxiety, and for once allowed the light-hearted girl who still lurked inside her to bubble to the surface to meet the newly discovered boy in Luke.

He grinned down at her. 'You've got ash on your face.'

'Much?' Marion wiped haphazard fingers round her mouth and chin. 'Is that better?'

His grin widened. 'You've made it worse. You've given yourself a Charlie Chaplin moustache. I must say, it suited him much better than it does you. Hold still. Let me wipe it off for you.'

His request for her permission was purely token. Without waiting for her either to give or to withhold it he took her chin firmly in the fingers of his one hand and tipped up her face towards him, and shaking out the folds of a pristine handkerchief with the other, he proceeded unhurriedly to wipe away the offending smears.

Marion quivered under his touch, and momentarily his hand stilled, his sensitive surgeon's fingers transmitting her reaction with the speed and accuracy of a radar probe.

For a brief second the blue eyes fired, and Marion blinked under the blaze, and tried without conviction to tell herself that it was merely a reflection of the flames from the bonfire, and knew that it was not.

The knowledge sent bright colour rushing to her cheeks, and Luke's lips tilted as he watched the hot tide rise under his ministrations, but he continued to wipe away at the smudge with the same unhurried efficiency that was the hallmark of all his actions, enjoying her confusion, she realised with a flash of indignation that prodded her into speech.

'The fire—it's hot,' she mumbled, using it as an excuse for her fiery cheeks, and instantly wished she had not spoken as his lips parted, and strong white teeth gleamed in silent laughter, mocking her embarrassment, and taunting her because she knew, and he knew, that the real cause was that strange chemistry which flows sometimes between a man and a woman, regardless of whether they wish it or not.

Definitely Marion did not, and, not for the first time when she was with Luke, fear pricked her. If the chemistry exploded, the subsequent smoke might cast a cloud that would be darker than any smudge made by bonfire wood ash, and not nearly so simple to disperse. She said hurriedly, 'Surely the moustache must be gone by now.'

Luke studied the results of his handiwork critically. 'Mmm, all gone,' he pronounced. 'I must say I prefer you as Maid Marion, rather than Charlie Chaplin in disguise.'

Marion's pulses jerked. Her husband used to call her Maid Marion. She should have resented Luke copying him, however unwittingly, but for some reason she did not, and the lack was in itself a warning.

Perhaps it was the witchery of the leaping flames from the bonfire that was having such an odd effect upon her. The long tongues of fire cast flickering red light that played about the clean-cut planes of Luke's face with an almost Satanic effect, and Marion watched it come and go with a fearful fascination.

The silence lengthened between them, and with an effort she dragged her eyes away, and stumbled into speech.

'I'm not a maid any more. I'm a working mum, remember?'

Flippant words, that dispelled the witchery, and brought back the harsh reality of every day, and Marion felt as if she could almost hear the brittle link between herself and Luke splinter into a thousand unmendable pieces.

With its going, the carefree girl and boy disappeared as well, and in their place the man and the woman were back, with the same question hovering, unasked and unanswerable, between them.

Luke said quietly, 'So you are.'

His voice was flat and Marion's spirits zeroed to match it, and she greeted Sue's arrival with an uprush of relief as her next-door neighbour bustled up with her family in tow, and started distributing leaflets with the explanation, 'The headmaster asked us to help spread these around. He's holding a meeting in the school hall at the weekend, and wants everybody who can come along to be there. He's going to try to resurrect the campaign to get a bypass built round the town. It folded before because they couldn't agree on the route, or something.'

'This time, they *have* to agree.' Marion latched on the new, safe topic eagerly. 'Nothing must be allowed to jeopardise the lives of children.'

'Our lives are in peril right here and now if that man doesn't stop prodding the bonfire. Just look at those sparks. Stand back, twins.' Sue shepherded her offspring to a safer distance as the enthusiastic stoker fed yet more wood into the heart of the already roaring fire, and sent up a veritable galaxy of sparks floating high into the surrounding darkness.

'They're as pretty as the fireworks.' Marion watched them fly, and changed her mind promptly when a still glowing ember descended upon the cowl collar of her sweater and began to smoulder its way into the cloth.

'Oh, my goodness, it'll burn a hole right through.' Frantically she flapped at the bit to remove it from her collar, but the ribbed material was elastic, and sprang the hot ember the other way, landing it underneath against the delicate skin of her neck.

'Ouch!' Desperately she dived her hand beneath her collar, but Luke's fingers got there first.

'Stand still a minute while I hook it out.'

'You'll burn your fingers.'

A surgeon could not afford to burn his sensitive finger-ends, but Marion's protest fell on deaf ears. Stilling her frantic wriggles with one hand, Luke deftly hooked out the offending ember. In his haste to get rid of it, his fingers caught on the delicate gold chain hung round Marion's neck, and the sharp tug tightened the links against her skin, and she put up her hands and exclaimed, 'Be careful. You'll break it.'

The small gold wedding ring dangling on the end of the chain flicked into view and landed in the middle of Luke's palm, and Marion's eyes, wide and shocked, flew to his face, reading in his expression first puzzlement and then dawning comprehension as his eyes went from her ring to the damaged knuckle of her ring finger.

She gritted through set teeth, 'I told you two and two don't always make five.'

'Marion, I'm sorry...'

Was he sorry for nearly breaking the chain or for misjudging her morals? Fury at his arrogant assumption that he had the right to judge her at all stung Marion into retaliation.

'You can keep your sorrow. I don't need it. I've had enough of my own.'

With trembling hands she snatched the ring back from his palm, and running her finger-ends along the length of the chain to make sure that it was still intact, she stuffed her treasure back out of sight under her sweater.

'We're going home now, Marion,' Sue called across to her. 'The twins are getting droopy.'

'I'll come with you.' Marion grasped at the opportunity to extricate herself from Luke's company.

He contradicted her sharply. 'I brought you here, and I'm taking you back home.'

'There's no need. You said you wanted to see the headmaster before you left.'

'We can both see him when we come to the meeting at the weekend.'

He did not ask Marion if she wanted to attend the meeting, he simply took it for granted that she would. Did he also take it for granted that she would go with him? Marion felt as if the jaws of a trap were beginning to close round her, and spiritedly she underlined her right to choose for herself.

'I haven't decided yet whether I'll go or not. I might have something else on.'

'You *must* attend. You're critical to any debate about the bypass, in case there are dissenters among the audience.'

'Who could argue against the need for a bypass, after Robbie's accident?'

Luke shot her a sardonic look. 'Self-interest can be a powerful lobby. Look what a battle I'm having to keep the Flying Squad on the road, even though the board know how many lives it's saved already.'

'That's different. It's you fighting against the hospital board. This time, it will be the entire school staff and the parents, all in league together. Among all that lot, my presence isn't likely to make much difference. In any case, you'll be the VIP, as the town's top surgeon. You, and the headmaster.'

'You're the mother whose child nearly lost his life in the accident.'

It was unanswerable. Luke was unanswerable, and seemingly unstoppable. Marion felt the familiar acid taste of defeat in her mouth that ended all her battles with him. Even the natural forces seemed to be aligned against her.

Sue called out, 'We're off now. Are you coming, Marion?'

And the bonfire chose just that moment to send a puff of smoke straight into Marion's face that choked her return call, 'Yes, I...' and sent her into a paroxysm of coughing that left her helpless to contradict when Luke called back,

'You go on, Sue. I'll take Marion home.'

Her eyes streamed and Marion dabbed at them furiously, but by the time her sight and breathing were restored to normal, Sue and her family had disappeared among the crowd, and as she did not know where their car was parked, it was already useless for Marion to go in search of them.

She spluttered into speech. 'I want to go home. I've had enough of the bonfire.'

She had had more than enough of Luke's dictatorial attitude, that constantly pushed her into situations over which she had no control but over which Luke remained supreme, and her exasperation showed in the look she flashed at him as he said mildly, 'Why so eager to go back home? The night's young yet.'

'There's my uniform to wash, and a meal to get, and...'

'Your uniform can't have got soiled today, we haven't been called out. Which only leaves the meal. What have you got that will take so long to cook?'

'Cook? At this time in the evening, after being on duty all day? You must be joking.'

'You can't exist on snacks.'

'I shan't expire from malnutrition if I make do with something on toast for one night.'

Luke must by now be needing his own missed dinner, and if he took her home right away she could use the excuse of not delaying him as the perfect reason to avoid inviting him in.

He sabotaged her wishful thinking with a decisive, 'We'll go to a pub I know. It serves excellent meals.'

'You're not obliged to feed me, just because you gave me a lift to the bonfire.'

'I am obliged, if you insist upon neglecting yourself.' Meeting her rebellious look he enlarged, 'Until I can get reserve teams trained to cover both shifts of the Flying Squad, I can't risk any one member of our present contingent falling sick. If you don't eat properly, you can't work properly.'

It was her work he was concerned about, and not her wellbeing. Marion's lips curled. 'What reserves? Don't you mean a male replacement for me?'

In spite of herself the bitterness showed through, and Marion felt Luke's eyes lance downwards on to her head, but deliberately she kept it lowered as she paced beside him, thankful for the comparative darkness of the school yard as they made their way towards the parked Jaguar, made even darker in contrast to the lurid light of the bonfire they had left behind.

'I meant exactly what I said. I need two full reserve teams to stand by, in case accident or illness depletes the present complement at any time.'

'We're a pretty healthy lot.'

'None of us is immune. As a nurse, you should know that. The worst of the winter is still to come, and it only needs a couple of us to go down with flu to put the Flying Squad off the road.'

Marion made a silent vow not to allow herself to succumb to even the slightest sneeze as Luke settled her into the passenger seat and slid behind the wheel beside her, and she tried hard to keep the anxiety out of her voice as she asked, 'Tell me more about the reserve teams. This is the first I've heard about them.'

It made her distinctly uneasy to learn about them now. If Luke was able to attract a man with the right qualifications, there was no doubt he would use him on the present team, and relegate her, Marion, to the reserve team with all speed.

Certainly on the reserve team she would still be able to continue to work at the General, which was the prime reason for her applying for her present job, but uneasily she knew that the original reason was now overshadowed by another, equally important one.

If she was put on a reserve team, she would no longer be working with Luke, only for him.

It was professional pride, of course, and nothing more, she assured herself stoutly. A very natural human one-upmanship at being the first in the field, and working as right-hand woman to the instigator of the Flying Squad.

And wanting it to stay that way.

Marion tried unsuccessfully to quell the hollow feeling inside her, but it would not go away, and she had to force herself to ask, 'Have you got anyone lined up yet?'

'Mmm.' Luke beamed his attention on negotiating the long car out of the school gateway and on to the narrow, cobbled streets beyond, and was silent as he pointed its bonnet out of town.

Marion sat rigid in her seat beside him. She longed to shout at him, 'Tell me. Tell me.' And knew that if she did she would be wasting her breath, because Luke would tell her nothing until he was good and ready, and then only what he thought it was good for her to know.

Her fingers balled into nervous fists in her lap, and she was hardly aware of what route the car was taking. The powerful headlights sliced twin beams through the darkness ahead of them, taking over the task of the street lamps as they exchanged cobbled streets for country roads.

Her tension was such that, when Luke finally spoke, she jumped violently, and pretended another fit of coughing to hide her nervous state.

He said casually, 'I've got a short list lined up. I should have the final selection made by the end of the week.'

Reaction set in, and Marion went limp. Her mouth was dry, and the palms of her hands felt wet, and she felt as if she would roll from side to side with rag-doll helplessness had not the efficient seat-belt held her in place in the luxurious embrace of the seat, as the car rolled smoothly round the snake-like bends of the country lane.

Her pent-up breath exhaled in a long sigh. Exit Sister Rowley. She knew the time had to come, and now it had. Grasping at pride to help her, she forced herself to respond, and her voice came through in a hoarse croak from her parched throat.

'With more staff to train, there won't be any more days without a practice call-out.'

Her words trailed into silence. There was nothing more to say. Fixedly she stared ahead through the windscreen, but even without looking at him she felt Luke's eyes swivel to search her face.

'You sound as if you've still got smoke in your throat. It won't be long now before you can have a drink and wash it clear. We're nearly there.'

'There' came towards them rapidly. Lights glinted, the scattered pinpricks indicating a village, until a larger pool of light revealed itself as a hostelry.

'The Cooper's Arms.' Marion read the sign out loud as Luke slowed the car, and nudged the bonnet in between two fat barrels that marked the entrance to the car park, and she wondered desperately how she would manage to swallow either food or drink.

Nemesis had struck, and she must take the blow with as much dignity as she could muster, because Luke must not suspect that it was a blow at all, but fervently she wished the agony need not be prolonged by having to endure a meal in his company.

She took deep draughts of the cold night air to steady her as she got out of the car, and Luke said, 'Hold on to me. The car park hasn't been tarmacked yet, and the hardcore makes for rough walking,' and immediately made things worse by putting his arm round her waist in case she should stumble on the uneven surface.

The feel of his arm was torment about her, and she longed to fling herself free, and contrarily longed to hug it to her, and thought raggedly, 'If I go on like this, the quicker I join the reserve team and part company with Luke the better, so that I can get myself sorted out.'

Her emotions were a bewildering mixture of contradictions that yo-yoed her moods between highs and lows like a crazy barometer trying to keep track of an electric storm.

Only one thing was certain, and Marion grasped at it to console her. Whatever she was suffering from, it could not be love. She had known love once, and would surely recognise it again.

The emotions which Luke aroused in her were the very opposite of love. Although she respected him as a colleague, she detested him as a man. But somewhere in between the two was this inexplicable attraction that, once she no longer worked with him and saw him every day, must surely fade.

He steered her towards the studded oak door beneath the swinging inn sign, and reaching out a long arm he grasped the iron handle and reverted to her earlier comment.

'There's no way we'll be able to train the reserve teams ourselves. We're much too busy. With the workload we're carrying at the moment, our own practice sessions are as much as we can cope with.'

We... The word acted like a shot in the arm, and Marion's leaden spirits began to soar, behaving in their usual erratic manner apropos of Luke, and impatiently Marion slapped them into submission and forced her voice to a cool, professional interest.

'What then?'

'I've arranged for all the reserves to attend a seminar in Amsterdam before they join us. I've got a connection with one of the hospitals over there. They've set up a scheme similar to our own Flying Squad, and they've offered to take on the newcomers and train them, in return for an exchange session for their own people later on.'

Amsterdam. Of course, Luke was a member of the van Zelt family. That would explain the connection, but the fact hardly registered in Marion's mind beside the significance of his plans to send the reserve teams to be trained in Holland.

They meant reprieve for herself. Even if a fully qualified man was among the newcomers, for the time being at least she could not be replaced on Luke's team.

He would still need her, Marion, to work alongside him on the Flying Squad.

CHAPTER FOUR

AGAINST all Marion's expectations, conversation flowed easily between them when she and Luke sat down.

The landlord ushered them to a table beside a glowing log fire, with the cheerful invitation, 'You might as well have it to yourself. There won't be many customers in this evening. Everyone's gone out to the bonfires.'

Perhaps it was the warmth of their welcome, or perhaps it was the superb food, or a combination of both, that made the cosy intimacy which Marion had dreaded seem to fall into place so naturally.

They talked in a desultory fashion about this and that as they waited for the meal to arrive. Luke said, not looking at Marion, 'Have you been on your own for long?'

His eyes brooded on the fire, following the lazy tongues of flame as they curled round the fresh logs with which the landlord had replenished the hearth. His voice was quiet, incurious even, as if he was merely filling in the gap with conversation until it was time to eat. As if he did not really care about Marion's answer, or even whether she answered or not.

It made it easy for her to reply, equally quietly, 'David was killed five months before Robbie was born. He was an engineer on the oil rigs. There was an accident.'

'Tough on you.'

Luke spoke to the fire, still not looking at her, and Marion was grateful for the mini-privacy as she confessed, 'What followed made me tough. I had to learn to cope alone, and fast.'

Luke turned his head, then, and looked at her. A long, considering look, that probed beneath the calm exterior, and read the struggles, and the failures, and the triumphs of those early, difficult years, like the damaged finger that could no longer wear the precious wedding ring. And knew, disconcertingly, that the toughness was only on the surface.

Marion's eyes dropped away from the searching blue eyes, suddenly unable to meet them, unwilling for the X-ray vision to search out any more of her secrets, including the one she had this very moment discovered for herself.

With a sense of shock, she realised that this was the very first time that she had been able to talk about the past without its hurting. It was as if the warmth from the fire purged her of all pain, and enabled her to reply with complete honesty, 'In a way I suppose I was lucky. At least I didn't have to worry about being able to keep on the house. David's job was dangerous, and he knew it, and he insured his life, so that afterwards the mortgage was paid off automatically. It still left the everyday bills to cope with, of course, but with Robbie to work for, I managed somehow.'

With everything to buy for a new baby it had been a struggle, and Luke's thoughtful nod encompassed that as well, but all he said was, 'Your house is well placed for getting to the General easily.'

'Do you have far to come?' Deftly Marion turned the conversation, and to her relief Luke followed her lead.

'I live at the Mill House on the other side of town. The place is much too big for me really, but I keep one wing as a base for the family when they need to fore-gather for meetings in England.'

Marion knew the Mill House by sight. Who in Farnmere did not? It was on the exclusive side of town. The side for Posh People, Sue called it, flippantly describing the district with its large houses, each lying in its own well tended grounds, not many miles in distance but light-years away in life-style from her own street of neat, semi-detached dwellings with the pocket-handkerchief gardens that obliged Marion to take Robbie to the local park whenever he wanted to ride his bicycle.

A vague memory about the Mill House teased her mind as she recalled the beautifully restored building lying on the banks of the Farn, with the mill-wheel still turning in obedience to the current of the river. She had pointed it out to Robbie, and explained its original purpose to the child, the last time they passed that way on an outing with Sue in the car.

The elusive memory failed to identify itself, and it faded as she said, 'It's a long way out from the General, but in your type of car you shouldn't notice the extra miles.'

Briefly, the contrast between the luxurious comfort of the Jaguar and her own twice-daily battle at the busy bus stops introduced a grating note, but before it had time to impinge and spoil the atmosphere, the landlord returned and began to bustle about with serving dishes, and perforce the conversation lapsed.

Luke had chosen the meal without reference to her, an extension of his customary dictatorial attitude which always aroused Marion's anger, but tonight, for some reason, it did not.

A peculiar languor stole over her, bringing with it a sense of relaxation that must be an illusion, and a transitory one at that, because in Luke's company she could never allow her guard to slip completely.

But while the feeling persisted, Marion grasped at the temporary release it afforded her, and thrust away the certainty that tomorrow everything would be back to normal again, including, no doubt, their abrasive relationship.

When the food arrived, she discovered Luke's choice to be impeccable. Meat marinated in wine to a succulent tenderness melted in Marion's mouth, and when Luke commented, 'I thought you'd enjoy this dish. It's a specialty here,' she was forced to admit,

'It's delicious.'

The vegetables exuded a flavour that could only be attained by being freshly garden-picked, although the sauces which accompanied the dish were subtly flavoured with spices whose origin conjured up names of exotic places far from an English village.

The mixture of fruits in the creamy sweet which followed was a similar, far-flung cropping, and Marion ate slowly, savouring each mouthful. Luke smiled at her appreciation, and she stopped eating and watched him, savouring instead the rare sweetness of his smile, crooked by the injury sustained in the train crash, so that Marion's fingers knew an urge to smooth away the slight scar that puckered the one corner of his mouth, resenting the despoilment of the otherwise perfectly cut lips.

This was madness. It must be something in the spices, or the strange fruits, or... Whatever it was, she must take a grip on herself before the effects began to show.

Marion tightened the grip on her spoon instead, and dug it fiercely into the remains of her sweet, and Luke's smile broadened, misunderstanding her movement, and he laughed and said, 'What say we take their chef with us when we go to Amsterdam in the spring?'

His words jerked Marion back to reality. 'We?' she exclaimed.

'Yes. As soon as we've got the reserve teams operational, I want us all to benefit from the Dutch seminar. They're just as keen to come over to us, eventually, and exchange experiences. Both the Flying Squads are in their infancy, and the more we can learn from one another the better.'

Marion's enjoyment in her meal faded. 'How long shall we have to be away?'

'*Have* to be away?' he echoed. 'You sound as if you don't want to go.'

'Of course I want to go. It's just that ... Robbie ...'

She could not possibly go away and leave Robbie while he was in hospital. It would be too cruel. It was not as if his grandparents were alive and able to take charge of him. The nearest relatives they had were at the other end of the world, and she and Robbie only had each other.

Marion swallowed hard. She could not expect Luke to understand her dilemma. On his own admission, he was not a parent, so he could not possibly share her feelings. And even if he had been, it would be different for him, because he had brothers and sisters on whom he could rely, while she was out on a limb on her own.

She had never felt more alone. Pride refused to allow her to beg for favours, especially from Luke, and the silence tightened her nerves, destroying the last vestiges of relaxation. The landlord broke it by bringing coffee, and when they were alone again together, Luke said, 'Robbie will be running about again, long before we go to Holland. The next seminar isn't until April. It's a comprehensive one. There isn't the urgency to get the reserve teams on the road that there was initially to get the first teams trained, and the reserves will be over there for a number of weeks.'

'Weeks?' Marion's wide eyes reflected her dismay. 'Even when Robbie's back on his feet again, I don't know if Sue would be prepared to take responsibility for him completely for so long.'

Depression descended on her. To attend the seminar in Holland was the chance of a lifetime, professionally. It would consolidate her own right to a place on Luke's team as nothing else could do. To refuse to go would give him the perfect excuse to get rid of her. But how could she possibly leave Robbie for weeks at a time?

Across the width of the table she could feel Luke's impatience mount at her negative response, and her dormant anger flared into life. What right had he to criticise her, when he had never been in the same difficulty himself, and was never likely to be? She braced herself to meet his wrath.

When he spoke, the sheer unexpectedness of his words pricked her defiance like a balloon.

'Why not bring Robbie along with you? I can arrange for my sister to look after him. She loves children, and one more won't make any difference to her. Her own three are bilingual, so Robbie won't feel stranded, and it would be a splendid holiday, to make up for his being in hospital now. He might even pick up a bit of the language while he's over there.'

'Why should you do this for us?'

In spite of Luke taking her out tonight, their relationship was a purely professional one, as was his relationship with Robbie, that of surgeon and patient. So why? Her creased forehead showed her puzzlement.

Luke lifted his shoulders in the merest indication of a shrug. 'As I said, if you don't eat you can't work. By the same token, you can't put your mind fully to your work if you're distracted by personal worries, so...'

So to make sure that her work did not fall one whit below his impossibly exacting standards, he was prepared to take charge of her private life and manipulate it to his own selfish ends.

Even to manipulate Robbie.

The prospect fanned Marion's resentment into full flame. Luke's arrogance was unbelievable. During working hours she was obliged to accept his dominance over her movements. That was unavoidable, since he was her boss. But she was not prepared to allow him to control her son in the same high-handed manner.

She hedged in a tight voice, 'I'll see, when the time comes.' Emphasising that the decision was hers alone. 'Robbie might be happier staying with Sue, if she's prepared to take him.'

'At least tell Robbie about it, and give him the opportunity to choose for himself. If he takes to the idea of coming along, it will give him something exciting to look forward to. Anything like that can make a tremendous difference to a child's recovery.'

He did not add that, as a nurse, she should be aware of the difference. He did not need to. His tone said it for him, and the implied criticism stung. As a nurse she was fully aware of it, but stubbornly Marion fought back, retaining the right to be the one to make all decisions affecting her son.

If she told Robbie at all, it would be when she decided, and not at Luke's dictation. Through thinned lips she repeated, 'I said, I'll see.'

Black brows drew together over blue eyes gone suddenly hard, as hard and unyielding as the diamonds that fostered his family's wealth. Luke said curtly, 'Have it your own way.'

Electric tension crackled between them, destroying the earlier, easy atmosphere, and when he asked, 'More coffee?' Marion shook her head. He offered her brandy, and she refused that, too, as did Luke himself, waving away the landlord's poised bottle with, 'Not for me, thanks. I'm driving.'

Soon afterwards, they took their leave. The drive back was made in a tight silence. Speech would have been superfluous. The car was already loaded with unspoken demand, and silent defiance, and when Luke drew to a halt at her gate, he made no attempt to get out of the car and take her key and open the front door for her as he had done before. Instead he pushed up his sweater sleeve, consulted his wristwatch, and said, 'I'll see you on duty tomorrow. I'll just make it back in time for late ward rounds.'

He dimissed Marion's stammered thanks for the meal with a wave of his hand, and she turned away from the car and walked along the short garden path, conscious with every step of a niggling sense of loss at the omission, and angry with herself for feeling it.

Luke's silent regard from the depths of the car pierced her shoulder-blades, and made her fingers fumble with the latch key and have difficulty in fitting it into the lock.

She gritted her teeth, and muttered, 'Go *in*, won't you?' because if she struggled for much longer, Luke would think she was making a deliberate play so that he would come and open it for her. The possibility stuck in her throat so that she hardly noticed the pain when the force of her efforts rammed the key home with disconcerting suddenness, and her fingers met the hard wood of the door with a knuckle-bruising thump.

The moment she shut it behind her, the big car pulled smoothly away from the pavement. Against her will, Marion turned and watched it go, and condemned her feet for not carrying her straight along the hall and into the kitchen, as was her wont when she first got indoors.

She could see the Jaguar quite clearly through the frosted glass, *ergo* Luke must be able to see her outline against the same glass, and he would know that she was waiting and watching for him to leave, and she lashed herself for feeding his already inflated ego by remaining where she was until he chose to depart.

The tail-light disappeared at the end of the street, releasing her, and she turned slowly away from the door. There was no real point in her going to the kitchen anyway, tonight. There was no meal to cook, and no uniform to wash. No Robbie to look in on when she went upstairs, either.

Before the 'no-ness' could get at her, and turn the suddenly threatening prick behind her eyes into humiliating tears, she blinked rapidly and forced herself upstairs to bed.

Whatever today had been like, tomorrow would bring work, and routine, and she had to be fit and rested in order to withstand the new day.

To withstand Luke.

A restless hour later she wished she had accepted his offer of a brandy, if only to make her sleep. In spite of her physical tiredness, her mind refused to rest.

Like a video film, it insisted upon a playback of the evening just past. Snatches of conversation. Luke's deep voice talking, for once, not about work, but about himself. His family. His home, the Mill House.

Again that faint, elusive memory stirred in the back of Marion's mind, teasing her. There was something about the Mill House, or its environs, which she felt she ought to recall, and could not.

Her mind drifted back, to the mixed joy and anguish of Robbie's birth, and having to cope alone with a new baby, which excluded her from everything else going on round her at that time.

It was then that the initial attempt to get a bypass built round the town had been raised, and failed.

Of course. That was why the Mill House had seemed to be so significant, when Luke mentioned where he lived. And why the memory had been so faint.

She had been too occupied with her own affairs to take part in that long-ago campaign for a bypass, even though she was fully behind its aims, which were to drive the road across land on the other side of the town.

Through the Posh People's district, she realised now, and remembered with a cynical grimace the fierce opposition the proposal had aroused at the time from the wealthy residents, that had gone a long way towards making the early campaign founder.

Had Luke been one of those residents, all those years ago? she wondered with a frown. Had he lived in the Mill House then, and opposed the bypass just as fiercely as his neighbours had done?

A mental calculation left Marion in no doubt that, had the scheme gone ahead, some of the considerable acreage attached to the Mill House, that ran along the banks of the Farn, and belonged by tradition to the old mill, would have been swallowed up in the process.

Had Luke opposed the route then, and in the face of recent events was he now unwilling to own up to his part in the collapse of the earlier campaign? And if so, what would be his stance at the meeting on the same subject this coming weekend, if the route put forward was the same as it had been before?

Luke made no reference to it, nor to their evening out together, when they met the following morning.

Marion caught the early bus to the hospital so that she could spend time with Robbie before she went on duty, and found Luke already sitting beside her son's cot when she walked through the ward door.

An irrational panic grabbed her. She wanted to back out again, to pretend she had not arrived. She would come back later, when...

But later was too late. She had taken only half a step backwards when Robbie sang out excitedly, 'Come and look at my new conker, Mum. It's great. It's bigger than the one Adam had, and Luke says it's a one-er.'

The child's sharp eyes had been watching out for her, and caught the movement of the ward door, and there was no escape as Luke turned and watched her advance across the polished floor.

His movement caused something to swing pendulum-wise in his hand, attracting Marion's attention, and she blinked. Surely, not another conker? Not during ward rounds?

Robbie chirped, 'We've been having a match, and I've won. Luke showed me how to swing my conker without hitting my thumb.'

'Nice of him,' Marion mumbled.

Luke in mufti, producing a conker from his pocket, had been surprise enough. But Luke playing conkers while dressed in a starched white coat, every inch a senior consultant from his highly polished, hand-made shoes, to his immaculately groomed hair, was difficult to take in.

'It's excellent therapy,' he pointed out drily, and Marion flushed, and his eyes held her rising colour until she longed to close her own to shut out the piercing blue.

'Shall we play another game, to show Mum?'

Robbie saved her. Luke smiled, and shook his head, and rising to his feet he carefully tied the string of his own conker on to the complicated structure of wires and pulleys that held Robbie's leg in traction, so that the small sphere swung easily within the child's reach as he lay in the cot.

'It's time I went to see my other patients. But I'll leave you my conker to practise with.'

'Mine's a one-er too. What if I break yours?'

'Here are some replacements. I've drilled holes through them, ready for the string. If mine breaks, all that you have to do is ask a nurse to untie the string, and thread it through one of the fresh conkers. Don't put the spares in your mouth, though, will you? Promise?'

'I wouldn't anyway. Mum told me not to. She says they're poisonous.'

Marion's look at Luke flashed a green warning, 'Don't you dare to contradict me,' and twin blue devils taunted back, 'You can't stop me, if I want to.'

Marion's hands clenched into tight fists at her sides, and then opened again just as suddenly with an urgent longing to slap her tormentor, when he agreed mildly, 'Your mother's quite right. I'm glad you're grown-up enough to do as she says. Now I really must go. Put in as much practice as you can with your conker, and see if you can beat me again next time.'

'Gosh, this is great. Look, I can make your conker fly.'

With an aim which Marion envied, Robbie struck out with his own missile and sent the one which Luke had hung on to the wire swinging round and round at the end of its string like a crazy fairground ride.

The child's ready imagination took wing along with it.

'Look, Mum, it's an aeroplane. I can pretend I'm in an aeroplane. Brrrmmmmmm...'

A sixth sense warned Marion of the danger, split seconds before Luke spoke. She began urgently, 'Don't tell...'

Even as she uttered the words, she knew she was wasting her breath. The devils stopped dancing and were replaced by a steely intent that warned Marion he was going to tell, whatever she said. She moved swiftly to try to circumvent him.

She turned her back on the surgeon and bent over the cot, as if by putting her physical presence between the man and the child she could blot out what Luke was going to say.

After what she had said last night, if Luke told Robbie about the trip to Holland, she would...she would...

He spoke, and her spine tingled with anger at each slow, deliberate word.

'You might be riding on an aeroplane for real, soon, Robbie. Not just pretend.'

'Gosh, do you really mean it? Where to? When?'

'Ask your mother. She'll tell you.'

Without another glance at Marion, he swung on his heel and quit the room, leaving her glaring helplessly at his retreating back.

She might have known that Luke would not give in so easily. She could not accuse him of telling Robbie about the trip to Holland himself. Instead, cynically, he had put her in the position where she had no option but to do the telling herself.

Fiercely Marion condemned Luke under her breath, but Robbie's eager questioning demanded that she produce some sort of explanation to satisfy him. Helplessly she gazed down at her son, and knew that it would take a tougher resolution than she possessed to deny the bright anticipation shining up at her from the small freckled face on the pillow.

Luke had known it too, and used the knowledge to trap her to his own advantage.

'Where to, Mum? When?'

'To Holland. But nothing has actually been settled yet,' she said cautiously. 'And if it is, it won't happen until long after Christmas.'

Craftily she drew a red herring across her explanation, but the annual excitement of Christmas paled before this new and thrilling prospect, and Robbie refused to be sidetracked until Marion cut across his insistent questioning with a firm, 'I've told you, nothing's been decided yet, so don't get all worked up over something that might not happen,' but to her dismay Robbie's enthusiasm waived such a minor detail.

'Wait till I tell the twins. Won't they wish they could come too? They haven't been in an aeroplane, not ever. Can I learn some words in Dutch before we go, Mum?'

Doubtless Luke could teach him those as well, Marion thought wrathfully, but she had no intention of putting herself under any further obligation to the surgeon by suggesting it.

'I'll see if the library has got a book,' she hedged, and went on duty a few minutes later with a deep frown marking her forehead.

Far from affording her peace of mind, as Luke had suggested, his interference was causing her still more problems to add to the pile she had already got, and he could not expect her to thank him for it.

A sharp lowering of the temperature overnight, and consequent black ice on the roads, soon began to cause her problems of a different kind.

A steady stream of skid-accident victims began to crowd into Casualty from the early-morning commuters, and perforce Marion had to put her own problems to one side in the face of the more immediate emergencies which demanded her attention.

She had time to snatch only ten minutes of her lunch-break with Robbie when the buzzer in her pocket blared out a summons.

Wheeep! Wheeep! Wheeeeep!

'If Luke's calling us out on a practice, on top of the sort of morning I've just had, I'll slay him,' she muttered furiously as she raced downstairs, only to find when she got outside that it was a bona-fide emergency after all.

She piled into the vehicle seconds ahead of Luke, and before he had time to slam the door behind him as he joined her on the bench seat they were heading out of the hospital gates on their way to a multiple pile-up at the junction of two main roads on the edge of town.

That night, a light dusting of snow added to the hazards and kept the staff working at full stretch for the rest of that week, which in a way made things easier for

Marion, because when she and Luke were together there was no time for personal discussion between them. Even when they met at Robbie's cot-side their visits were curtailed because of the mounting workload that left Marion drained when she finally went off duty after lunch on the Saturday.

She wanted to do nothing except wallow in a hot bath, and then stick up her weary feet for the rest of the day, but that was not possible because the meeting in the school hall was laid on for that evening, and for Robbie's sake she had to be there.

Not simply because Luke said she must attend.

Sue popped round for the latest news of Robbie when she got home, and Marion said tiredly, 'I hope the meeting won't go on forever tonight. I feel shattered. What time do you want me to be ready?'

Sue looked surprised. 'Luke told me he was taking you.'

'You two must have a hotline between you. He said nothing to me.'

'I suppose he took it for granted.'

'Like he takes a good many other things for granted,' Marion snapped, and was instantly contrite. 'Sue, I'm sorry. I didn't mean to sound bad-tempered. It's just . . .'

'Surely you've seen Luke at the hospital? I thought he'd have told you.'

That is just what he would have done, if he had thought about it. Told her. Not asked. Marion bit back another sharp retort, and admitted, 'We haven't had time to talk about anything but work. The Flying Squad has been called out three times today, and we've had the scrum of Casualty to deal with as well, in between. When I left, Luke was still working in theatre with the latest batch of admissions.'

'He never stops, does he?'

'Never.' Marion's clipped tone did not reflect Sue's admiration, and she was aware of her neighbour's questioning glance, but she could not help it.

Luke was spreading the tentacles of his dictatorship to her neighbour, as well as round Robbie. How far would he go if she did not stop him, and soon?

'You're not exactly his number-one fan, are you?' Sue quizzed, and Marion pulled a face.

'He's far too domineering for my liking. I have to put up with it while I'm on duty, but his control doesn't extend to my off-duty hours. Now he's trying to dictate to me what I should do with Robbie when we go to a seminar in Amsterdam in April.'

'That sounds exciting. Tell me.'

'That's exactly what Luke did. Told me, I mean. He didn't think it was necessary to ask. He even got it worked out where to take Robbie while I'm in Holland, and expected me to meekly accept all his arrangements without a word of protest.' Tiredness, frustration and anger spilled over, and Marion poured her discontent into Sue's sympathetic ears. 'That's what I wanted to ask you about, Sue,' she finished hopefully. 'Would you be prepared to look after Robbie while I'm away?'

'Not in April, I can't.' Sue dashed her hopes with such a quick refusal that it was Marion's turn to look surprised, and it returned the bite to her voice when she said,

'Has Luke got at you about this, too? Is he the reason you're refusing?'

'He'd better not be.' Sue laughed out loud. 'Hubby would have something to say about it, if he were. Seriously, though, simmer down and listen. I've got some news, too. How would you like to be godmother to our new arrival in April?'

'New arrival? Oh, Sue, I'm so pleased for you. Anything I can do to help...'

'We haven't managed our timing very well, either of us,' Sue replied ruefully. 'Junior will be due just about when you're away in Holland. Any other time I'd have had Robbie with pleasure, you know that. But during April I've got to fix up a rota of baby-sitters myself, for the twins. By the time you and Robbie get back, though, I should be in orbit again, and taking the twins to school as usual, so we can revert to our normal routine then.'

Which was small consolation to Marion in her present dilemma.

No matter how she tried to play it down, each time she saw Robbie he chattered incessantly about the longed-for air trip, unknowingly tightening the screw on his mother until she longed to beg him, 'Let it rest, do.'

The subject allowed her no rest. Her mind constantly ping-ponged between her own longing to attend the seminar, the need to accommodate her small son if she did, and the equally urgent need not to give in to Luke.

Her problem was still unresolved when Luke called for her early, before Sue was ready to start out for the meeting at the school.

Making sure I shan't hitch a lift with Sue and escape his clutches, Marion told herself uncharitably, and knew compunction when Luke walked into the brightly lit hallway and she saw the fine-drawn lines of tiredness marking his face, that even his iron self-control was unable to erase.

Instead of the sharp comment that rose to her lips, Marion surprised herself by asking, 'Have you eaten?'

'Yes. I finished operating a couple of hours ago. But it was touch and go with that young motorcyclist, so I stayed around until his condition stabilised a bit. I used the time to shower and eat a meal in the canteen. It gave me the chance to get my second wind, ready for this evening.'

Obviously he anticipated a battle at the meeting, but the break had had the same therapeutic effect upon Marion, and she felt ready for whatever might come when Luke drove them both the short distance to the school soon afterwards.

'We're early,' she remarked. 'Perhaps we'll be able to get somewhere near the front. I'd like to be able to see and hear clearly everything that goes on.'

'You'll be able to do both without any trouble. You're on the platform, along with me.'

'On the platform with the VIPs? Oh, no!'

'I told you, as Robbie's mother, you're our star exhibit. You must play it for all it's worth, if you want the bypass to go ahead.'

'You didn't say anything to me about being on the platform. Why didn't you warn me?' Marion wailed.

'Warn you? What for?'

'So that I could dress in something different, for goodness' sake.' For once, Marion's essential femininity was in the ascendant, and her indignation was quite genuine. 'I've put on the same trouser-suit and sweater that I came in to the bonfire.'

She had dressed casually in a gesture of defiance to Luke, and now it had rebounded on her, and irrationally she blamed her companion for her discomfiture.

'Women!' Luke's expression struggled between amusement and exasperation. 'What on earth do clothes matter? I thought for a moment you might have wanted time to prepare a speech.'

'Don't be silly.' Marion felt rendered speechless by the mere prospect.

'It's you who is being silly. What you had on for the bonfire is an excellent choice.' His lips crooked briefly. 'There are likely to be just as many sparks flying about tonight. In any case, you look fine to me, just as you are.'

His tone was briskly reassuring, and Marion sent him a suspicious look. She surprised a glint in his eyes that said he really meant it, and she felt a traitorous thrill run through her as he took her by the arm and walked her beside him through the crowd that was already gathered in the school hall, towards the semicircle of chairs set out ready on the dais at one end.

Luke was still in his consultant's garb of perfectly tailored suit, immaculate shirt and silk tie, and he looked tall and distinguished as he shook hands with the waiting dignitaries, and in no way disconcerted by her casual attire.

Marion forgot about it herself within minutes of the meeting getting off the ground.

The headmaster opened the proceedings with a brief speech, the mayor replied on behalf of the Town Council who were there in force, along with the police chief and the local MP.

The formalities over, the borough architect unrolled a large map, on which the suggested route of the bypass was marked by a bold red stripe, like a scarlet ribbon snaking across the parchment.

The colour proved prophetic.

The route was identical with the one that had been put forward years previously, and within minutes the hall became a noisy battleground of conflicting opinions as to its suitability.

Marion viewed the behaviour of the audience in total astonishment. This was the first large public meeting she had ever attended, and her expectations of a reasoned debate were rudely shattered.

Verbal flak began to fly as the audience split into two opposing camps, those for and those against the proposed route. The necessity for the bypass was not at issue. Everyone agreed that it was necessary, but there their accord ceased.

'It's started a civil war,' Marion exclaimed in an aside to Luke. 'I thought everyone would want the bypass.'

'They do. But not through their own backyard.'

'If they go on like this, the whole project is going to fold, as it did before. It mustn't. I won't let it.'

The prospect was too much for Marion. Visions of Robbie's accident repeating itself haunted her. She jumped to her feet, and two bright spots of colour flamed on either cheekbone, vying with her rich auburn hair, against which her eyes glittered with the light of battle. Her shrill cry cut across the uproar in the hall like a hot knife through butter.

'What does it matter where the bypass goes, so long as it's built?'

The noise cut off abruptly, and the silence could be felt as every eye turned in Marion's direction, but she was too wrought up to care. The spirit that had carried her through the last few years came to her aid now, and she accused her hearers passionately.

'While you're all arguing about which route the road should take, another child might be injured, or even killed. Just as my own little boy so nearly was.'

The memory of Robbie's stained grey school sock sticking out from under the huge lorry wheel returned with vivid clarity, and she felt suddenly sick.

Tiredness, overcharged emotion, and the thought of what might have been and so nearly was, took the bright colour from her cheeks, and paled them to the background colour of the parchment map.

She sat down abruptly. She was aware of Luke's eyes searching her face, but she did not care about that for the moment either. With the attention of the whole room riveted upon her, what did one more pair of eyes matter?

The only thing that mattered to her was that the town should—*must*—get the bypass, and nothing and nobody must be allowed to stand in its way.

Marion clenched her hands on her lap and fought for self-control, and with quick opportunism the head-master stepped into the silence and grabbed at the chance to restore order.

'I'm sure we all sympathise with Mrs Rowley's dis-tress, and we're all delighted to hear that her little boy is progressing satisfactorily.'

A low murmur united his audience again, and swiftly he built on the ground gained. 'Can we have silence for a moment please, to hear the views of our guests, who have all, I'm glad to say, agreed to be on the committee if the bypass scheme goes ahead.'

'*When* the bypass scheme goes ahead,' Marion put in fiercely. She had not agreed to be on any committee. Perhaps Luke had done the agreeing for her, without consulting her, in his usual arbitrary manner.

The headmaster looked startled by her attack, and hurriedly passed the buck. 'Perhaps the Chief Constable would care to give us his comments.'

The comments of the Chief Constable endeared him to Marion for life.

'I agree entirely with Mrs Rowley. It is imperative that Farnmere has a bypass, and the sooner the better. Don't you agree, Councillor?' he asked the man who sat next to him.

'Up to a point. While I sympathise with the lady's feelings, the view she puts forward is very simplistic. There are many things to be taken into consideration.'

'What things?' Marion flashed. 'If my view is sim-plistic, what could be simpler than a choice between life and death, because that's basically what we're all talking about. Or are we?'

Self-interest can be a powerful lobby.

Luke's words came back to her forcefully, and she eyed the councillor with disfavour. His appearance was unprepossessing. The heavy-jowled jaw and ostentatious tie-clip provided a stark contrast to the uniform of the Chief Constable and Luke's sparse frame on his other side. She pursued her attack, feeling rather like a small terrier barking at a huge bull mastiff.

'You don't have to deal with the consequences of road accidents. We do.'

'Naturally not. I run the hardware store in town.'

Marion made a mental note to obtain all her household gadgets in future from somewhere else, and appealed directly to Luke for support.

'Luke...that is, Mr Challoner.' She felt herself go bright red, and stiffened against the councillor's beady stare. 'We have to deal with the road accidents at first hand. We're at the sharp end of any disaster, and the results are far from pretty. Ask Mr Challoner.' The name rolled glibly off her tongue this time, she thought proudly, and went on, 'He said himself that we are the ones who have to sweep up the bits. If there are any left,' she finished significantly.

'Mr Challoner?' The headmaster skilfully passed the baton on, and Luke rose to his feet.

His presence dominated the meeting. Even the coughs and shuffles from the audience ceased. Most of the families represented had at some time needed his help at the hospital, and their silence was a signal mark of their respect.

He said quietly but clearly, making no effort to raise his voice—having no need in the deep, anticipatory hush that awaited his words—'There is absolutely no question about the need for a bypass round Farnmere. I think we are all agreed on that. The need is urgent, and vital. Lives are at risk daily until such a road is built and in operation.'

Hurray! Luke was backing her to the hilt. Marion's shining look applauded him. She need not have had any fears about the stance he would take, after all. He was completely on her side.

'What I do question, however, is the proposed route for the new road.'

'It's the identical route that was put forward before,' the architect pointed out. 'In fact, this is the same map that was used then.'

'Exactly. And the reasons against the road being built along that route are just as strong now as they were then. I agree wholeheartedly that we need the bypass. I totally oppose the route you have chosen.'

CHAPTER FIVE

How *could* Luke?

How dared he turn traitor, and oppose the bypass? Marion stared at him, stunned. There could only be one reason, of course. The proposed route would take the road across part of his property.

Only a very small part, but it was enough to realise her worst fears about him. Out of the huge acreage attached to the Mill House, he was not prepared to sacrifice even a small amount in order to help preserve the lives of Farnmere's citizens.

She had wondered if Luke had been among the objectors to the original scheme, had tried to visualise him raising objections this time, but in her heart of hearts, after what had happened to Robbie, she had not seriously believed that he would.

She knew differently now. Totally opposed. That was how he declared himself. And total opposition from Luke usually spelled ignominious defeat for the other camp.

Marion's mind burned. She became aware of the architect enquiring, pan-faced, 'Perhaps Mr Challoner can suggest an alternative route, that would be as suitable for the road as the one I've marked out on the map.'

'I can suggest a very much better one.'

He would, Marion fulminated. But better for whom? For Luke, or for the town?

'Such as?'

'Surely it should be obvious? Route the bypass across the common.'

The proverbial pin would have reverberated through the silence that met his suggestion. The common was Farnmere's playground. It was sacrosanct. To suggest building anything on it at all was tantamount to blasphemy in the eyes of its citizens. The whole room seemed to draw in a collective breath, and then suddenly everybody began to talk at once.

'The common belongs to the town...'

'...green belt land...'

'...threat to wildlife...'

'...erosion of recreational facilities...'

Luke viewed his audience with an impatient tightness in his expression that Marion had come to know well. The eminent surgeon was not accustomed to other people disagreeing with his pronouncements, and she waited with derisive interest to see how he would handle the situation.

With confident authority, as she should have guessed.

Luke waited for the volley of objections to rattle into near silence, then he held up his hand sharply. The instant hush brought him a look of startled envy from the headmaster, but Luke ignored the VIPs and concentrated his attention on the main body of the audience in the hall.

He spoke to them in a calm, reasoning tone that must have cost him an immense effort, Marion thought cynically. Luke was more accustomed to steam-rollering his point of view over that of his opponents, supremely confident that his way must always be the best one, rather than appealing to the reasoning powers of other people, which he probably doubted anyway.

'Because the common belongs to the town, that fact alone will eliminate the need for prolonged negotiations over land ownership.'

His land, among others. But he was careful not to say so. Marion's lips curled as she listened.

'Ask yourselves which is more important to you? Losing a small slice of the common, or losing lives?' Luke threw his challenge at them, and went on to demolish the rest of their objections with ruthless efficiency.

'It is a recorded fact that wildlife deliberately chooses to colonise the banks of motorways, because they can obtain more peace there than on open areas of land which are used more and more for recreational purposes. Also, the common is on the side of the river farthest from the town. If the bypass is built on the town side of the river, in line with the architect's map, it will mean that anyone wanting to use the common will have to cross the bypass to get there. Think about the dangers that will represent.'

'You have a point there,' the Chief Constable applauded, and Luke shot him a look that said it was one that should have been considered before, and went on forcefully,

'I say, keep the bypass on the other side of the river. The Farn is the town's natural defence against unchecked development, and we breach it at our peril.'

'All very dramatic,' Marion scoffed as the meeting broke up and the audience went on its way, the various factions still arguing hotly over the further fuel which Luke had added to their fire.

'It's in the best interests of both safety and the town itself,' Luke told her crisply, accelerating the Jaguar clear of the clutter of departing vehicles.

'Are you sure it's the safety of the town you're interested in?' Marion gravelled. 'That you haven't got another motive? A more personal one?'

'You mean, the possibility of losing a slice of my own land?' Typically, he met her challenge head on, and not for the first time Marion found his bluntness disconcerting, but she allowed her silence to answer for her as the car travelled the short distance back to her house and slid to a stop outside her front gate. Hastily she pushed open the door without waiting for Luke to perform the service for her.

She had already extracted her door-key from her bag and had it gripped in her hand, but Luke's long stride took him round the bonnet of the car before she could prise herself free from the embrace of the low seat and regain her feet.

'Allow me.' His eyes mocked her haste to get away, and he bent and took both her hands in his and pulled her to her feet, and too late Marion knew that he must feel her door-key in her fingers.

He extracted it smoothly into his own, and pulled her upright in front of him, and she raised defensive eyes to his. His narrow glance glinted back at her in the subdued light of the street lamp, and she retreated behind hastily dropped lashes, and muttered, 'It's getting late.'

She slid round him and almost ran across the pavement to the front gate. Suddenly the backlash of the day hit her. All the work weariness, followed by the tension and anger and disillusion of the meeting—disillusion with Luke—caught up with her in a rush, and she could not continue any argument with him tonight.

On Monday she would return to the fray, when her off-duty weekend would leave her in better shape to hold her own, but not tonight. She stumbled on a broken corner of a concrete slab that was second in line along her front path, and which she kept meaning to have replaced and had not got round to, and tried wildly to think up some excuse not to invite Luke in for the coffee which courtesy demanded.

He followed hard on her heels along the path, neatly circumventing the broken slab, fitted her key into the door lock and said, 'You need to get that slab fixed before you break your neck on it.'

'I'm going to, as soon as I can get round to it.'

If there had been a man about the house, it would have been done automatically by now, but there was no man, as Luke knew full well, and she could not attend to everything at once, on her own.

Anger rose in her at his criticism. He had no right to criticise. No right to comment, even. But it stung nevertheless, and the smart made her lash back, forgetting her tiredness.

'You can't deny that losing your land is your real motive in blocking the bypass. You don't want the road in your own backyard either.' Bitterly she threw his own words back in his face.

'What do a few acres of land matter?' he interrupted her impatiently. He left the key dangling in the lock and transferred his hands to her shoulders, as if he might be tempted to shake her into seeing his point of view. Marion stiffened against his hold, and he said tightly, 'Can't you see what I'm trying to do?'

'All I can see is that you're opposing the bypass and if enough people follow your lead, the whole scheme will fall flat on its face, as it did before. And I won't let it. I won't let *you*, do you hear?' she cried fiercely. 'I won't...'

Her voice choked dangerously on the edge of tears, and she felt his fingers tighten on her shoulders, and thought wildly, If he dares to shake me, I'll scream.

'I'm trying to do what's best for the people of the town, and for the town itself,' he growled, and Marion flared,

'Prove it. You can't.'

'I can't stop arguing with you tonight, that's for sure. I want to check on that young motorcyclist again, before I go home.'

'That for an excuse,' she sneered.

'No excuse, and you know it.'

She did. She had good reason to know Luke's dedication to his patients, frequently at the cost of his own rest, and instantly felt ashamed, but she smothered the feeling, and Luke went on, 'It'll be easy enough to prove, if you'd open your mind to the other side of the argument, and listen to my reasons.'

Marion bridled. 'Reasons, or excuses? I'll take some convincing, after your performance this evening.'

'Then tomorrow, I'll convince you.'

'I'm off duty tomorrow.'

'Which is why you're free to come out with me.'

'I'm seeing Robbie.'

'Not until the afternoon visiting-hours. The staff on the children's ward are up to full strength again, and they won't need your help to look after him, and he's being moved out to the big ward tomorrow, so that will have to be an end to his special privileges. The parents of the other children who are on the mend have to abide by the regulation visiting-hours, so...'

So in future Marion must do the same. Because Luke said so. He was not only taking charge of Robbie, he was trying to prise her apart from her son.

'You—you...' she choked, and Luke cut across with a curt:

'You know the rules, Marion. Just because you're a member of staff it doesn't give you leave to bend them. Perhaps *because* you're a member of staff, it's important for the morale of the other children and their parents that you mustn't be seen to bend them.'

He was quite right, of course. Just as he always was, but Marion's white, set face hated him for it.

'Robbie will wonder why I don't come in the morning.'

The slight quaver in her voice was checked instantly, but Luke's tone gentled, rasping her pride because it told her that he had noticed.

'Robbie knows you won't be coming in to see him until the afternoon.'

'*You* told him, I suppose?'

It should have been she herself who told Robbie, breaking the news to him, and consoling him at the same time, just as she had always done. Luke replied evenly, 'I told him before I came off duty tonight. It wasn't decided until quite late to move him, which is why I wasn't able to warn you. One of the other children is going convalescent a few days early, and it will leave room in the big ward for Robbie's cot. You want him to be well enough to move out of special care, don't you?'

'Of course I do, but...'

'He took the news like a champ. He said to tell you to have a lie-in tomorrow morning, and don't forget his joined-up numbers book when you go to see him tomorrow afternoon.'

A tight band seemed to grip Marion's throat. Joining up numbers to make pictures was a new craze since Robbie had started school. She managed with difficulty, 'The book's already in my bag, for tomorrow.'

'So, have your lie-in. But be ready when I call for you at ten o'clock. That is, if you're not afraid to come with me, in case I might change your mind about the route for the bypass. Is that it? Are you afraid?'

That was only a part of it. There was something else about which Marion was even more afraid of changing her mind. Dismayed, she discovered that she was afraid of changing her mind about Luke.

In spite of her anger against him, it was folly to underestimate the strength of his virile attraction, which each time she saw him seemed to grow stronger.

'I...I...' she began, but Luke gave her no time to think up another excuse to avoid meeting him.

With a quick movement he pulled her to him, bent his head over her, and brushed his lips lightly across her own. For a brief second, so brief that she was not sure whether it was merely in her own imagination, his grip seemed to grow tighter on her shoulders, straining her even more closely against him, but before the sensation had time to register he pushed her away, and in a voice that sounded oddly rough he bade her, 'Don't forget. Ten o'clock tomorrow, on the dot. If you're not ready, I'll carry you off even if you're still in your nightie.'

He would be quite capable of carrying out his threat. For a tantalising moment Marion's mind toyed with the idea of opening the door to his knock clad only in négligé, and if she did, what would be the outcome...

'See you,' he taunted, and the broad set of his shoulders and the proud carriage of his head silhouetted against the night sky drew her eyes irresistibly as he strode away along the path. The front gate clicked shut behind him and his long length jack-knifed into the driving-seat of the Jaguar, and automatically Marion raised her hand in a wave as the car pulled away along the street. The tail-lights disappeared, and it seemed as if a light went out in her. Angrily Marion snubbed her thoughts back under control and scolded herself, 'Sister Rowley, you must have taken leave of your senses.'

Or are you just coming back to them? a small voice inside her enquired innocently, and with a gasp Marion flung open the front door and fled upstairs two at a time, stuffing her hands over her ears in a vain attempt to shut out the sound of the voice, but unable to blot out its chuckle that said it knew the message had been clearly received and understood.

What to wear posed a problem the next morning.

Luke had not said where he intended to take her, but any bid to convince her that the bypass must be routed over the common must surely entail a walk across it?

Visions of Luke's loose, athletic stride sent Marion hunting for a pair of flat-heeled suede lace-ups which she had not worn since last winter. Her trouser-suit and sweater were the obvious choice for such an outing, but if she put on that outfit again, Luke would think she had got nothing else to wear.

A sally out into the garden presented a crisp golden morning, sunny but not too cold, and with hardly any cloud, and returning for a thoughtful review of her not too plentiful wardrobe, although what she did possess was all of good quality, Marion thought thankfully, she chose an all-round pleated skirt in fine brown wool with a sweater to match, and topped it with a warmly lined trench-style mac with comfortably deep pockets that would hold house-keys and hanky, and save her the trouble of having to carry a bag, which she detested. When she was walking, she liked to have her arms free.

Free for what? the small voice inside her spoke up again, and as if in answer Luke's now familiar brisk rat-tat sounded on the door knocker.

'Be quiet,' Marion ground out at the voice savagely, and pulled open the front door.

'I didn't think I was making all that much noise.' Luke quirked an enquiring eyebrow at her. 'Do your neighbours lie in until lunchtime on Sundays?'

'I didn't mean you.'

Marion blushed a fiery red. Luke looked as if he had been up with the dawn. He probably had. She knew he would have done ward rounds, even although it was his day off, but his clear-skinned, fresh-eyed look might have come straight from the shower.

'Who then?'

'What . . . er . . . oh, one of the neighbour's dogs was barking,' Marion improvised hastily, dragging her mind back from the way Luke looked, with difficulty.

'Funny. I didn't hear a dog barking.'

His laughing look showed that he disbelieved her, but to Marion's relief he did not pursue the matter as he helped her into the car with the usual courtesy that seemed to be so much a part of him, even when he was angry with her.

Luke was dressed in the same outfit which he had worn to go to the bonfire, confirming her assumption that they would be walking the common. Had he worn the same clothes himself, assuming that she would wear her trouser-suit again because she had no change of mufti? Humiliation returned the colour to her cheeks, and she shook her head as if to shake away her thoughts.

It was all too complicated, and it was a sin to spoil such a beautiful morning worrying about such thing as clothes when stolen hours spent walking were all too rare, especially those made brighter by scarce winter sunshine.

Or by Luke's company?

Marion sighed sharply, exasperated by the persistence of the voice,

'Something bothering you?' Luke heard the sigh, and slanted her a questioning look.

'No . . . yes.' Marion sat upright in her seat, noticing for the first time the direction in which the car was heading. 'I thought we were going to the common.'

'Disappointed?'

The common was well know as a rendezvous for every courting couple in the town, as Luke must be fully aware, and his question taunted her and posed another, and brought hot flags of embarrassment to Marion's cheeks.

'I . . . you . . .'

He chuckled. 'I don't know whether you look prettier when you're angry or when you blush.'

'Don't change the subject,' she snapped.

'OK. I asked if you were disa . . .'

'I don't mean *that* subject.'

Even the tips of her ears felt as if they were on fire to match her hair, and Marion felt she could cheerfully have slapped Luke. She made her voice repressive and could then have slapped herself when it came out sounding prim.

'I thought we were going to the common to study the route for the new bypass.'

'How very dull.' He grinned wickedly, caught Marion's vitriolic look and almost, but not quite, managed to straighten his lips.

Maybe the curl still remaining had something to do with the scar that puckered their one corner. With this infuriating man, it was never possible to be sure.

'So, I've decided to liven up our study a bit,' he announced with suitable gravity.

'How?' Her voice was loaded with suspicion, and provoked a return of the grin.

'By taking a bird's-eye view of the landscape,' he told her mysteriously, and refused to explain any further, leaving Marion fuming in silence as the big car ate up several more effortless miles.

Pride refused to allow her to question Luke, as he obviously hoped she would simply for the pleasure of refusing to answer her. She scorned herself for the effort it took her to deny him that pleasure, but she could not restrain her surprise when they came to the local flying club airfield, and instead of driving straight past it, Luke turned the nose of the car and took them right through the entrance gates and drew up in front of the clubhouse.

The explanation of his 'bird's-eye view of the landscape' hit Marion at the same time as her eyes lit on the parked helicopter.

'You're not taking me up in that thing?' she exploded forcefully.

The transparent dome of the 'copter, built for observation purposes, looked as fragile as a soap bubble, and just about as insecure. Other aircraft were parked near to the clubhouse, but a horrid premonition told Marion that this must be the one Luke had in mind.

Her fears were confirmed when he stopped the car quite close to it, and taunted, 'Scared?'

She was, very. But, fortunately for the sake of her pride, at this moment she felt totally incapable of answering him. The bottom seemed to drop out of her stomach, leaving nothing to receive her wordless swallow when Luke helped her out of the car to stand beside him on the tarmac on legs that suddenly felt like jelly.

His keen eyes raked her face, and read the reason for her silence, and he pressed, 'You want the bypass, don't you?'

'You know I do, but...'

How much sacrifice was reasonable to achieve what she wanted? Surely there must be another, less terrifying way to survey the landscape? Marion had never wholly overcome her dislike of flying in conventional aircraft, and the prospect of leaving the ground in such flimsy-looking transport frankly appalled her.

'This is the quickest way to get an overall view of the whole area at once,' Luke insisted. 'It beats map-reading hands down. Come and meet Alun, the pilot.'

He steered her towards a fair, curly-headed giant who ambled down the club house steps towards them, and who must surely be far too large to ride in such a flimsy craft.

Alun grinned at Marion cheerfully, as he shook hands. 'You don't like the look of my kite,' he guessed from her expression.

'It looks a bit—er—delicate.'

Marion hastily retrieved her hand from a bone-crushing grip that made the same description apply to her fingers, but the pilot appeared to be in no way put out by her uncomplimentary opinion of his aircraft.

'Most people feel the same way when they first set eyes on her. It's the transparent observation bubble that does it. Makes you feel as if you're sitting outside on the wings. Only there aren't any wings.' Marion's rueful grimace said she would feel a lot safer if there were, and Alun laughed. 'You'll change your mind once we're airborne. Everybody does.'

Marion did not expect to number herself among the converts, but, pinned between the sardonic challenge of Luke's blue stare and the cheerful optimism of the pilot, she could not confess her cowardice, and forced her reluctant feet to accompany the two men to the helicopter.

Alun strapped her into the front seat beside his own, and enquired with a callous lack of sensitivity, 'Do you want the door left open, or closed?'

'Closed,' Marion shuddered, through teeth clenched tight to prevent them from chattering. Not that the door made a lot of difference. The view through the transparent material was so clear that there might as well not have been a door there at all. Marion tried ineffectually to ignore Luke's derisive grin as he took the seat immediately behind her, his greater height enabling him to see over her shoulder with ease.

The clatter of the rotor blades drowned her involuntary gasp as the helicopter lifted off, leaving her ill-used stomach behind, and they were airborne, and the sky was a blue canopy above them, the ground like a living map underneath their feet, the traffic as small as Robbie's toy cars, crawling along ribbon roads.

From behind her, Luke's hands somehow found their way on to Marion's shoulders, and she felt herself go rigid and then relax in spite of herself as the surgeon began expertly to massage away the tension of fear from the muscles at the back of her neck, his thumb a teasing rider across the delicate vertebrae at the top of her spine.

He leaned forward in his seat, and his breath zephyred her ear. 'Are you OK?'

The tension came back, but this time it had a different cause. The thumb traced lines of fire up and down, up and down, electrifying her whole body until Marion felt as if she were soaring way, way up, without any help at all from the helicopter.

Her heart did a dizzy loop-the-loop inside her breast, and the unnatural gymnastics must have had an effect upon the colour in her cheeks, because Luke asked her again, with more concern this time, 'Are you OK?'

She was, and she was not, and how was she to reply when the ragged edges of her nerves did not know which answer applied to what? The thumb slowed and stopped its sensual stroking as he waited for her to speak.

With an immense effort, Marion reclaimed her scattered senses, and managed to force out, 'I—I'm fine. Really.'

She felt safe in the helicopter with Luke. And terribly unsafe. Their relationship was a mass of contradictions that grew more tangled each time they met.

And each time brought her a step closer to the brink of a void that was infinitely more terrifying than the one which lay beneath her feet at the moment, and against which there was no door to shield her, and no safety harness to prevent her from toppling over the edge.

The pilot turned with a broad smile and surveyed his erstwhile nervous passenger. 'Told you, didn't I?' he boasted, and asked Luke, 'What do you want to look at first?'

Marion let out her breath in a soundless poof of relief. Bless Alun for bringing her back to terra firma, and the reason they were here. She felt as if she had just made a three-point landing, or whatever applied to helicopters, and eagerly she rushed on to the nice, safe ground which the pilot offered.

'Didn't you say you wanted to go over the common, Luke?' she put in swiftly.

'That, and along the course of the river, and then circle back round the town itself,' Luke nodded.

Ten minutes ago, even five, such a prolonged tour would have dismayed Marion. Now, to her astonishment, she became so immersed in spotting familiar landmarks from this very unfamiliar angle, all of them assiduously pointed out by Luke, that fascination temporarily overlaid her earlier fears.

Luke produced two maps, one a scaled-down replica of the architect's original map, and the second one showing an alternative route for the bypass across the common over which they were flying. She expressed her surprise.

'The architect didn't mention that he'd got an alternative map.'

'He hadn't. I sketched this one myself, last night.'

He must have burned midnight oil to do so. Even Marion's untutored eyes could see that it exactly duplicated the scale of the architect's efforts, and the bold penmanship showed a grasp of the subject which widened her eyes.

Luke was, indeed, a man of many parts, and she seemed to learn about a new one every day.

He leaned forward and spread the maps across her lap, the better for her to follow where he pointed, and the move made his arms, one on either side of her seat, circle it and Marion at the same time, making it impossible for her to concentrate on the map and the things which Luke was trying to point out to her down on the ground to match.

'That's where the line of the road would run, roughly over where we're travelling now.'

'Oh, er, yes...I see.'

She lied. Her eyes refused to take in anything except the sight of the long, tanned finger pointing out the new route across the parchment, its closely manicured, filbert nail doing disturbing things to her metabolism as it traced the line marked in bold ink across the map.

The finger of a surgeon, or a musician, or... Distractedly Marion wondered if Luke played an instrument. Her own nerve-endings were reacting to his touch like harp strings plucked by the fingers of a master, and the music they echoed sounded in her ears like the magic of Pan pipes, drawing her towards him. Making her afraid.

She wondered confusedly if Luke could hear the echoes too, and hastily she switched her mind to where it should have been in the first place, and made a wild stab at a more intelligent contribution to the discussion.

'You've drawn the bypass farther over towards the edge of the common than I thought you would,' she said.

'There's no need to drive the road right through the middle of it and ruin the entire common. If the bypass is restricted to the edge, it will avoid all the problems of the marsh land nearer to the river, and still leave plenty of common land for—er—recreation.'

The sort of recreation which he suggested Marion might have been hoping for on their morning out? His deliberate pause goaded her and her lips tightened, and she felt her neck ache with the effort not to turn her head and glare back at him.

'End of the common coming up,' Alun sang out. 'I'm turning the kite back along the river, now.'

The river led to the Mill House. In spite of her intention to show it no special interest, it drew Marion's eyes like a magnet.

Seen from the rear, the grounds proved to be much more extensive than were apparent from the road view, which was the only part of it she had seen until now. Alun cruised the aircraft at a leisurely pace, and as they came above the Mill House, he hovered, barely moving, above it.

'Nice pad you've got there, Luke,' he drawled.

Emerald lawns ran down to the river bank, lovely to stroll along on a summer's evening. Was this, perhaps, where Luke unwound after a hard day at the hospital?

Steps led down to a boathouse and a small jetty, evidence of peaceful hours spent on the river when the weather was fine. Marion's eyes grew wistful as she looked down on it. Messing about in boats had been part of her own childhood, and the lure of them still lingered. Only the opportunity to indulge it was missing.

Sudden movement attracted her attention back to the Mill House itself. Someone was waving to them from the terrace. A girl. Alun saw her at the same time, and he brought the craft down lower in response to the greeting, and an uprush of irritability caught at Marion.

Why could he not have kept the aircraft at its previous height? Going up and down vertically made her feel as if she was in a lift, and her stomach resented the unaccustomed yo-yoing. She gulped it back into place, and stared at the girl, who came running down the terrace steps on to the lawn, as if she thought they might land there.

'Shall we?' Alun turned to Luke, evidently on the same wavelength, and Marion wondered at the surge of relief which shook her when Luke answered, 'No, there isn't time. Marion's got to be at the hospital at two, and I want to be back here in time for lunch.'

To eat, or to see the girl who was waving at them from below?

Sick disappointment took the place of the relief, which was just as illogical, because she had not expected Luke to give her a lift to the hospital when she went to visit

Robbie. Had she unconsciously hoped that he would? The depths of her disappointment said yes, and blamed the unknown girl for being its cause.

The down-draught from the 'copter rotors whipped the girl's clothes tightly against her body. Designer clothes, even at this distance it was possible to identify the style and fit as being a far cry from that offered by the racks of the department stores. They moulded the model-tall, willow-slender body as if the girl had been poured into them, their bright colours a perfect foil for the mane of flaxen hair that flowed about her shoulders, and glittered like silver in the winter sun.

Luke waved back; the wave removed his arms from round Marion, and she felt bereft, and blamed the girl for that as well. The force of her feelings shocked her. Resentment, and anger, and other less worthy emotions which she did not want to name, boiled in a witches' brew inside her, and she felt as if at any moment they might boil over, and blow the fuse of her self-control. She wondered what Alun's reaction would be if they did, and she suddenly started to scream at Luke.

She was being childish, but she could not help it. This was to have been her morning, with Luke. It had been, until the flaxen-haired girl intruded. Even though she was on the ground, and they were in the air, subtly her arrival had changed the atmosphere, robbing it of its intimacy.

Useless to tell herself that the girl was nothing to do with her. That Luke's private life was nothing to do with her. That she, herself, was here to do a job, and nothing more. The morning was spoilt, and the fear returned, and this time it was not only the fear of flying that assailed her.

'They got here, then?' Alun spoke above the increased clatter of the rotor blades as he took the helicopter back up again, and Luke answered,

'Not yet. The rest of them don't arrive until this evening. Rea was in London doing some shopping, so she came on early, by train.'

Vaguely Marion remembered that Luke had told her he kept the Mill House so that his family could have a base in England for their business meetings.

Family? Surely the girl did not belong in that category. At least, not yet... Luke's hair resembled jet, while the hair of the girl, who was still waving up at them, was as pale as a moonbeam. Had she come on ahead of the others, in order to spend the time alone with Luke?

Rea. The name was a dart, pricking Marion's mind. What was so special that had brought her to London to do her shopping, all the way from Holland, presuming that was where she lived?

The prick was followed by another, sharper one. Had Rea been trousseau-shopping?

A spear of sudden pain drove the colour from Marion's cheeks, blotting out the scenery below them so that she was hardly aware of the helicopter turning away from the river to cruise over the town. Through a blur she heard Luke's voice talk on, but only an occasional word made any sense to her.

'...architectural gem...tragedy to allow heavy traffic through...'

He leaned forward again to point out this and that on the map, but Marion's eyes were too blinded to see, and the feel of his arm round her again made the pain worse, and instead of soaring, her spirits felt so heavy that it was a wonder they did not threaten the safety of the aircraft.

How little she knew about Luke, even now. His interest in architecture was news to her. Would it be news to Rea also? Somehow, she doubted it. She could visualise Luke escorting the flaxen-haired girl through the town, pointing out to her the lovely old buildings, and regaling her with their history, as they walked and talked, arm in arm along the cobbled streets.

Who *was* Rea?

Marion longed to ask, but she bit back the question that trembled on the edge of her tongue, because suddenly she feared to know the answer.

It was not the identity of the other girl that tormented her, but another, more vital lack of information.

What was Rea, to Luke?

CHAPTER SIX

'MUM, you're not looking. You've drawn the line from six to eight, instead of six to seven, and it'll make the picture come out all wrong.'

With an effort, Marion dragged her attention back to the joined-up numbers book. 'I'm sorry, Robbie. I'll rub it out and start again.'

She wielded the eraser on top of the brightly striped pencil which went with the book, and dutifully re-routed the line to the correct number.

The picture that was beginning to emerge was of an aeroplane. It would be, she thought resignedly. It was as if, even in this small thing, Luke's influence was reaching out to keep the trip to Holland in the forefront of the child's mind, and at the same time to increase the pressure on her, and bend her to his will.

Difficult to resist when Robbie persisted, 'Will we fly in an aeroplane like that, when we go to Holland, Mum?'

'I've told you, we may not be going to Holland at all.'

'But Luke said . . .'

Maledictions on Luke! Under her breath Marion condemned the surgeon's interference to outer darkness, but, unaware that he was treading on forbidden ground, Robbie chatted happily on.

'Kevin's flown in an aeroplane. He says it's great.'

Kevin was the cheerful seven-year-old in the next bed, who refused to allow a bout of appendicitis to dampen his spirits, and swung his two years of superior knowledge of the world in front of Robbie's dazzled eyes.

'If you do fly in an aeroplane, it won't be until April, and that's four whole months away yet, so forget it for now. Christmas comes first.'

'Nurse says we'll be having a party, with crackers, and a cake with Father Christmas on top.'

'And it's only just over a fortnight away,' twinkled a passing nurse, and Marion groaned.

'I haven't even thought of Christmas shopping yet.'

Time had sped so swiftly since Robbie's accident that the near proximity of the season of goodwill had escaped her, and the nurse's reminder came as an unwelcome jolt.

'Are you going to write to Father Christmas?' She used it as a lure to distract Robbie from his fixation on the trip to Holland. 'I can post it on the way home, if you like,' she suggested craftily, hoping the letter might provide her with some clues for her non-existent shopping list.

'I'll start it while you're here, if you'll help me.' Falling for his mother's ploy, Robbie reached for a blank page of his scrapbook, and outflanked Marion's manoeuvre with his very first question. 'How do you spell "aeroplane", Mum?'

Marion twisted the painfully printed scrap of paper between her fingers, and fought back tears as she made her way outside, along with the other parents at the end of visiting-time.

The reminder of Christmas had touched her on the raw. It had been bad enough without her husband for the first few years, but there had always been Robbie. Until now...

This year, she would be completely on her own.

The next week gave her plenty of practice in that respect. She saw little of Luke, and nothing at all of him outside working-hours. The harsh weather eased into a muggy mildness, and with it came a drop in the number of road accidents, and consequently fewer calls on the services of the Flying Squad. And now she was restricted to visiting Robbie only during regulation hours, Marion did not meet the surgeon on the ward either.

Presumably, Luke was spending his leisure time with Rea.

The thought nagged, however much she tried to thrust it away from her, and the realisation that she missed Luke's company rankled.

'I must be going soft,' she scorned herself, and threw her energies into the neglected Christmas shopping. Talc for Sue, sweets for the twins, and...Marion fingered the toy airport which she had bought for Robbie.

It was a silent capitulation to Luke. Several tiny aircraft were parked outside the painted wooden passenger terminal. A small yellow tanker refuelled one plane with steps drawn up to its side as if it had just landed, and there was even a miniature helicopter on an octagonal landing-pad.

Abstractedly, Marion's forefinger turned the tiny rotor blades round and round. Robbie would love his gift, and each time he played with it, it would fuel his ambition to fly in a real aeroplane.

He was certain to show it to Luke when the surgeon visited him during ward rounds. She could almost hear the childish voice exclaim, 'Look what Mum gave me.' And Luke would look, and know that she had lowered her flag, and he had won. She would attend the seminar in Holland, and she would take Robbie along with her, just as he planned.

She need not tell Luke yet. She would hold on to her pride for as long as possible, but she had to confide in someone, and Sue provided the needed sympathetic ear when Marion returned from duty one evening.

Sue took her news with deflating calm. 'You couldn't let the opportunity pass you by, for your own sake and for Robbie's. You've come to the only possible decision.'

'I know. It's just that Luke always wins.'

'That man's a go-getter, if ever there was one,' Sue enthused, with cardinal lack of tact. 'Have you seen the evening paper yet?'

'No, I haven't had time to open it. Is there anything spectacular?'

'I'll say. There are two things which will interest you specially. Luke's got the agreement of the hospital board to allow the Flying Squad to become a permanent fixture at the hospital.'

'Never! The board gave him a year to prove its worth before they even considered it again, and you know what that means. It's a virtual death-warrant when it comes up for approval the second time round.'

'True as I sit here, Luke's won all hands down. Apparently there was this young motorcyclist who crashed the other day...'

'What, the one in intensive care? It's been touch and go with him, but Luke says he'll pull through now.'

'Thanks to the Flying Squad, and Luke, he'll pull through. And it's got the hospital board grovelling. Seems the young motorcyclist is the chairman of the board's grandson.'

'Wonders will never cease.'

'Let's hope your two-legged wonder doesn't,' Sue said drily. 'If Luke keeps this up, he could solve a lot of the town's problems.'

'Luke isn't *my* wonder.'

'He took you to the bonfire, didn't he? And to the public meeting? And then you went gallivanting round in a helicopter together.'

'We weren't gallivanting. And there were three of us in the helicopter. Alun was doing the piloting.' Marion hated the betraying blush that warmed her cheeks, as Luke's, 'Disappointed?' came back to taunt her.

Sue grinned at her rising colour. 'I believe you. Having the pilot along must have spoiled things.'

'There was nothing to spoil.'

'OK, keep your hair on, I was only teasing. Have a look at this.' Sue retrieved the local evening newspaper from a nearby chair, and spread it across the table between them. 'If the reporter has got things right, your wonder boy has settled the argument over the bypass, as well, without a blow being struck.'

'I don't believe it.' Marion's indignation spilled over. 'After dragging me miles across the town in that beastly helicopter and scaring me half to death, he's got no right to settle anything on his own. That was the whole idea of my going along on the flight in the first place, to get my agreement to routing the bypass over the common, so that we could join forces to fight it out at the next public meeting.'

It was inexpressibly galling to discover second-hand that Luke had dragged her on a wild-goose chase for nothing. Cynically, he had paid lip service to wanting her opinion, when all the time he had already had his own plans formed, and intended to carry them out whether she agreed with them or not.

'He's got no right to take off and do his own thing like this,' she fumed.

'Doesn't look as if Luke agrees with you.'

'That's just the trouble. He doesn't expect to have to agree with anyone. He thinks they should all come round to his way of thinking. I've got more right to a say in the new bypass than he has. It was my son who was injured. Everyone should have a voice in this, not just Luke. He's nothing but a petty dictator.'

'You might find that you agree with him after all, if you'll just stop shouting, and listen.' Reluctantly Marion subsided, and Sue went on, 'It seems as if Luke's managed to drive the Town Council into a corner, and there's no way they'll be able to wriggle out of it this time, once the local citizens clap eyes on this article.' She stabbed a jubilant finger at the two-inch headlines, and began to read from the report with relish.

'"Mr Challoner proposes that the central area of the town, with its cobbled streets and ancient buildings, be pedestrianised, and an imaginative campaign of advertising set up to encourage the tourist trade".'

'That will make sure he has the backing of the tradespeople,' Marion opined sourly. 'He's nothing if not a good tactician.'

'You malign him,' Sue remonstrated, and read on, '"The present school will be bulldozed to the ground. Mr Challoner described the building as a Victorian monstrosity and the only eyesore in an architectural gem".'

'What does he propose to do with the space?'

'Turn it into a car park. That would be a blessing,' Sue added with feeling. 'Parking is a nightmare on shopping-days.'

'And where are the children supposed to get their education, if Luke does away with the school?'

'According to this, Luke's offered to give some land to the town.'

'Oh, great! Land by the river, so that the children risk being drowned instead of being run over.'

'Give him credit for some sense, Marion,' Sue expostulated. 'Apparently Luke owns that large patch of open ground near to the centre of the town as well. It says here, "Mr Challoner has not only offered his land, but also a substantial trust fund to ensure that in future the new buildings will be exploited to the full, as a further-education and leisure centre, as well as a school." Aha, here comes the crunch,' Sue chuckled. 'Good for Luke!'

'Which means bad for someone else,' Marion muttered, and Sue frowned her into silence, and hurried on:

' "Mr Challoner's gift is made on three conditions. One: that the council pay the cost of building the new school. Two: that the bypass is routed across the outer edge of the common. And last, but far from least: that every Farnmere resident has the opportunity to vote for or against these proposals. A form for this purpose is printed at the bottom of the page, so get voting, folks, and post your forms to us, and we will appoint an independent team to count them and let the council know your decision".'

Sue pushed the paper aside, and gloated, 'Luke isn't driving through his own ideas without consultation after all. He's giving everyone a say in the matter, which is more than the council would have done. Luke Challoner isn't a tactician, he's a magician. If the residents vote for his proposals, and I can't see anyone opposing them, there won't be a thing the council can do about it. They'll have to go ahead or risk being voted out themselves.'

'Blackmail casts a powerful spell.'

'You're not being fair, Marion, and you know it. It needs someone to drive the authorities into action. The council's talked about the bypass for years, and done absolutely nothing about it, and look at the results. Robbie's lucky to be alive.'

Marion was being unfair, and unreasonable, and she did not care. She could not forgive Luke for going it alone without saying a word to her about his intentions, when he had used up a whole morning of her time in order to sort out a solution to the problem together.

It was galling to realise just how much that togetherness had meant. Or was it merely an excuse on Luke's part to get his own way, as usual, and force her to do something which he knew she did not want to?

Her ire showed when, for the first time in days, Luke
waylaid her as she was coming off duty the next evening.

'Short of company?' she asked tartly, and could have
bitten off her tongue for revealing her feelings, but the
words were out and she could not recall them.

It was a mere two days to Christmas, and was supposed to be the season of goodwill towards all men, but
she felt just the reverse towards this particular man. She
said, 'I can't stop. I want to go home and wrap up
Robbie's Christmas present,' when what she really
wanted to say was, 'Has Rea gone home and left you at
a loose end? Is that why you've decided I'm worth talking
to again?' but she did not quite dare.

Luke's eyes narrowed. 'Had a bad day?'

'Not particularly. Why?'

'You seem short on temper.'

Stalemate. They locked glances like two fencers, each
watching for an opening to administer the *coup de grâce*,
and Marion thought miserably, We're quarrelling.

It should not matter, but it did, and it was all inex-
tricably mixed up with Christmas, and missing Luke,
and a vision of moonlight-silver hair. When the silence
had stretched for too long, she drew in a difficult breath
and forced out, 'I'm glad you won. About the Flying
Squad, I mean, and the hospital board.'

'I would rather it had not happened this way.'

Marion nodded dumbly. She knew exactly what he
meant. Luke would rather have fought it out to the death
with the hospital board than that one hair of the young
motorcyclist should be harmed. On this count, at least,
they were on the same wavelength.

Watching her closely, Luke tuned in to another.

'I wanted to know what you thought about the plans
I put forward for the town and the bypass. Have you
voted on them?'

'Not yet.'

'Will you?'

'I don't know. I haven't made up my mind.'

Marion resented being pressurised. Her first, angry instinct had been to ignore the voting slip, but somehow she had not been able to bring herself to toss the newspaper into the pedal bin as usual when she finished reading it. It still lay, a silent rebuke to her tardiness, where Sue had left it on the kitchen table.

Luke growled, 'You're a stubborn, contrary female. It's your duty to vote, if not for my sake, then for Robbie's.'

It amounted to a royal command, and his arrogance flicked Marion's anger into life. She flared, 'Why should I vote? Why should I do anything for your sake? You used me to gain attention at the public meeting, because it was my child who was injured, but you didn't think it was necessary to discuss with me what you intended to do. As usual, you went your own way, and did your own thing, irrespective of other people. You just took me for a ride. Literally. That wretched helicopter didn't look as safe in the air as any self-respecting sparrow.' A hint of hysteria shrilled Marion's voice as she added, 'At least a sparrow's got wings.'

'I explained to you every single move that I intended to make, in detail, while we were hovering over the town.'

'I didn't hear you.'

'You must have done. You'd got your eyes fixed on the map all the while I was talking, following what I was saying. Alun heard me, so you must have done as well; you're not deaf.'

Suddenly Luke's voice grew rough, and before Marion could guess what he was about to do he reached under the hospital cloak she had thrown about her shoulders for warmth, and grasped her by the arms, and accused her, 'You kept your eyes fixed on the map because you were too scared to look down at the ground underneath us? Admit it.'

His eyes took in her mutinously tightened lips, and his expression changed, and softened. 'My poor little passenger. I thought you were agreeing with everything I said because you didn't argue against me as you usually do, and all the time you weren't taking in a single word I said because you were so scared of being up in the air, and probably hating me for forcing you to come up with me.'

His voice and his eyes were a question, and the tightening grip on her arms warned Marion that he would not be satisfied until she gave him an answer. With an effort she unlocked her lips, and stammered:

'Yes...no...I mean, I don't...'

She had not heard a word Luke said in the helicopter because her mind had been taken up with other things, like designer clothes on a model-tall body, and pale hair blowing in the wind. But it was less humiliating to allow Luke to think that it was fear of flying that caused her inattention than to blurt out the real reason, and Marion retained a defensive silence.

'You don't what?' he insisted.

'I...oh, nothing.'

'You must have meant something.' He reached under her chin with one finger, and tipped up her face to meet his and her ready colour rose, but when she tried to turn her head away, his palm cupped her face and forced her to meet his eyes.

'Tell me,' he commanded.

There was no escape. His fingers stroked sensuously along the slender line of her jaw, forcing the words out, and in desperation Marion blurted, 'I don't hate you...not much, anyway,' she back-tracked hurriedly as his eyes fired.

'That's something, I suppose.'

His lips took more, punctuating each word that murmured low against her mouth, transmitting what he said more as a vibration that echoed back into her own mouth, so that her senses felt the words and she did not need to listen.

'It was cruel of me to make you fly. But you were so fierce in your fight to get the bypass, not a bit like the quiet, self-contained Marion I knew, that I thought...'

'And I thought...' Marion stopped. It was better if she did not carry her thoughts to a conclusion, because not hating Luke left the way wide open to... She braked fiercely on her thoughts, as much for fear of where they might lead her as that Luke might read them too.

'Seems we were both on the wrong track with our thinking.' Luke's kiss changed, and deepened, and Marion's mouth pursed under his lips with the eager hunger of being offered an unexpected banquet. After an endless minute Luke raised his head, but his hands still held her close.

'It's time we stopped thinking and fighting, and called a truce,' he declared. 'It's Christmas. Listen.' He smiled, that sweet, crooked smile that had the power to make her heart take flight. 'The staff are having their first carol practice in the chapel.'

They stood and listened together as the high, sweet strains of 'Silent Night' floated across to them through the darkness, and Marion stirred in his hold.

'I was on my way to join them.'

'So was I. We'll go together.'

Marion blinked dazed eyes as she preceded Luke into the brightly lit chapel, and felt strangely unready to be confronted by the crowd of singers gathered there, who all too soon shattered the precious seconds of oneness between them with their stir and bustle, and called greetings.

The distinctive uniform which she and Luke still wore set them apart from the rest of the hospital staff and denied them anonymity among the crowd, and heads turned in their direction, curious, questioning, speculative.

The small building was warm with the packed ranks of singers, but Marion hugged her cloak tightly about her shoulders, instinctively using it as a shield against the curious stares.

The imprint of Luke's fingers where he had held her still burned like brands upon the soft flesh of her upper arms, and she knew an irrational fear that, if she removed the cloak, the marks might show through the thin stuff of her Flying Squad uniform. They sent warmth radiating through her body, a special, personal warmth, that no one else could share, and the cloak helped to hold on to the warmth for just a little longer.

Marion accepted a carol sheet from a porter, and took her place among the crowd as the conductor raised his baton to start the next carol.

'Once in Royal David's city...'

Her voice rose pure and sweet, and her spirits soared to join the notes, that so short a time before had been lower than low at the prospect of spending Christmas alone.

She knew a passing shock at their meteoric rise, but it disappeared in the enjoyment of the singing as Luke came to stand beside her, and his voice rose alongside her own, a strong, clear baritone that sent a thrill vibrating through her with his every note.

Startled, her eyes flew up to his face, and he caught her look, and his singing lips crooked into a smile. Marion smiled back, sealing their truce, and it seemed as if there were only the two of them singing together, their voices intertwining in a paean that mingled pleasure with a curious pain.

After the carol practice was over, Luke took her home. Marion lay back in the luxurious car seat and closed her eyes, feigning tiredness, but underneath the sheltering lids her mind worked furiously.

Away from the euphoria of the carol practice, she could no longer set aside her previous suspicions, and they returned in full force to torment her. Had Luke really sought her out in order to discover whether or not she had voted on his proposals for the bypass?

Or was he, as she suspected, using her for company because Rea was not available? Her pride cringed at the inevitable answer, and at the eagerness with which she had accepted his lift.

She had to believe Luke when he insisted that he had told her all about his plans, because there would be no point in his lying when she could so easily check with Alun. He had taken her agreement for granted when she had not argued with him, 'as usual'. The words were a barb. They made her sound shrewish. And I'm not, she denied to herself fiercely.

Was Rea?

She would never know. Of one thing only could she be certain. Luke was arrogant and domineering, and he expected everyone to bow to his will, and she, Marion, refused to be anyone's meek subject.

Perhaps that was the difference between auburn hair and flaxen, she mused. The spirit matched the hair. The one fiery and rebellious, and the other...

Insipid. The small voice was unrepentantly catty, and for once Marion did not attempt to silence it. How could she, when she was in complete agreement? It strengthened her confidence to invite Luke in when they stopped outside her front gate.

'Would you like to come in for a coffee?'

She despised herself for holding her breath until he answered, 'Make that two coffees. I'm parched after all

that singing,' and despised her accelerating pulse still
more as she agreed happily,

'Two it shall be,' and felt her blood sing in harmony
as she led the way along the hall to the kitchen, and
Luke filled the kettle while she got out the cups and
saucers, and it was all the same as it had been before.

But subtly different.

The steam from the kettle drifted wraith-like between
them, taking on the vague form of a slim body and
moonlight-silver hair, and Marion wondered if Luke
could see the resemblance too, or whether it was only
her own imagination that moulded the steam into a
ghostly form.

They sipped their coffee slowly, letting the dark aro-
matic liquid soak away the after-effects of the evening's
vocal efforts, but when Marion got up from her chair
to replenish their cups, Luke caught her to him, and
pulled her down on to his knee.

'You're beautiful, Marion.' His eyes devoured her upturned face, her eyes wide and green and enormous under
her tousled curls. 'Your eyes are as green as emeralds.'
He touched first one, and then the other, gently with his
lips.

'You know all about gems...'

Were Rea's eyes blue, perhaps pale, like her hair?

'I don't know enough about these.' He touched them
again lightly. 'Teach me more.'

He scooped her against him, and his lips left her eyes,
and lost their gentleness as they crushed her mouth,
parting its soft fullness with the passion of his kiss that
said he had little to learn, and everything to teach, if she
would become his pupil.

Marion quivered under his hold, shaken by the on-
slaught. Waves of sensation washed over her, and she
arched her head backwards the better to give access to

his lips as he sent them on a voyage of discovery down the long, slender column of her throat.

'...beautiful...' he groaned.

Her resistance wavered. She felt her body melt against his, and turned convulsively to raise her arms and clasp them round his neck, and the movement seemed to jolt Luke out of a trance. He shook his head like a swimmer coming up for air and, putting up his own hands, he pulled her arms down, almost savagely, and gravelled out, 'I've got to go.'

'B-but...your other cup of coffee?'

What did coffee matter? But it was all that Marion could think of to say, while she wondered distractedly if Luke too had felt the pale wraith drift between them in the kettle's steam. Had it crept into his mind even as he kissed her, and was the contrast with Rea more than he could bear? In that one moment of weakness, Marion would have been his if he had wanted her, and the memory of it burned in her like fire, destroying her.

'I don't want coffee. I don't want anything. Anything at all. Do you understand?'

Luke was shouting at her, blaming her for something, she did not know what. He thrust her off his lap, standing her roughly on her feet, and lurched unsteadily to his own as if he had drunk wine instead of coffee, and Marion knew that he had not. His eyes glittered like living coals in a face gone chalk-white under his tan, and he repeated harshly, 'I've got to go, I tell you. *Now.*'

She did not understand, and her outstretched hand pleaded with him to stay and explain, but he pushed it aside and strode past her, out of the kitchen and along the hall.

'Luke?'

Her cry was a whimper. Her legs trembled so that they could hardly support her, but she managed to force them in his wake along the hall.

'Luke?'

His answer was to slam the front door shut in her face, and, stunned, Marion stared through the glass at the tall, dark shadow striding away from her along the garden path.

The car door echoed the slam of the house door, and the Jaguar took off from the kerb with a screech of tyres, in a racing start that Marion had never known Luke to use before.

He avoided her the next day. It was Christmas Eve and, following tradition, Joy provided mince pies and cups of tea in her office for the Casualty department staff to enjoy whenever they had a spare moment during the day.

Marion was pouring herself a cup of tea when Luke put his head round the door. He did not see her at first, and greeted Joy with a cheerful, 'Happy Christmas, Sister,' and accepted his mince pie from a filled plate.

Marion turned with a gasp at the sound of his voice, and the unguarded movement directed the flow of tea from the spout on to her hand instead of into the cup. The scalding liquid stung, and with a yelp of pain she dropped the cup and saucer with a crash, and grabbed with both hands to prevent the filled pot from following them.

Joy rescued the pot and returned it to the safety of the table, and Marion bent hurriedly to pick up the shards from the floor, hiding her burning face from Luke's gaze, but she could not remain crouched there for ever. Once the wreckage was disposed of, she was obliged to turn and face Luke when Joy said, 'Have a cup of tea, Mr Challoner? Marion will pour one for you.'

Marion and Luke both spoke at once.

'You pour it, Joy. You're nearest the pot.'

'I can't stop for tea. I'll take my mince pie with me. I'm waiting for a phone call.'

Joy stared at the space which her visitor had occupied mere seconds before, and turned and threw Marion a thoughtful look. 'That's funny. When I saw him not five minutes ago, he said he was looking forward to spending his coffee break with us. Have you two quarrelled?'

'Yes' and 'No' would be equally true, and false, and to avoid getting entangled in reasons which she was not even sure of herself, Marion used a mouthful of mince pie, which she felt convinced would choke her, to mumble an indistinct reply which could be interpreted as either.

'What did you say?' Joy asked. 'I didn't hear...oh, hello, Doctor. Come and have a mince pie.'

Joy broke off as another member of staff arrived to take advantage of her hospitality, and hurriedly Marion made good her escape before she could be questioned further.

She saw no more of Luke until they gathered for the carol singing that evening. By pre-arrangement there were to be no practice calls for the Flying Squad on Christmas Eve. All the hospital services were on red alert ready to cope with any traumatic results of seasonal celebrations, which as the day wore on surprisingly failed to materialise.

The Casualty department remained strangely quiet too, and the bleeper in Marion's pocket maintained its silence. The duty doctor expressed the universal relief of the staff when he remarked, 'Good for the police! Their "don't drink and drive" campaign seems to be working. They threatened to crack down this year, and for once the silly asses who get tanked up and still think they're safe behind the wheel seem to have taken some notice of their warning.'

The relief expressed itself in the enthusiasm of their singing as the amateur choristers gathered together that evening to tour the wards, and take the Christmas message to patients and staff alike, and what their singing lacked in professionalism was more than made up for by the openly expressed pleasure with which it was received.

As senior consultant, Luke led the procession, and Marion was urged to walk beside him, not allowed to lose herself in the crowd as she wanted to, because their two distinctive uniforms marked them out as the natural choice to be at the front.

Luke accepted the place as his right. His arrogant right, Marion fumed, ignoring their truce that was no longer a truce, because Luke had broken it, so that she need not feel bound by it any longer, whether or not it was Christmas.

His strong baritone led them confidently from one carol to another, and the rest of the staff followed his lead happily, but it rubbed Marion raw that she was forced to pace beside him in outward acquiescence and inward rebellion, obliged to sing the carols he chose, and walk the route which he dictated.

Was it deliberate spite that made Luke avoid going into the children's ward? Twice he passed by the end of the corridor which led to it, and each time he glanced along it, and then walked on, and led the singers through another ward instead.

The first time, Marion cast a longing look along the corridor, and hesitated, but the others were coming on behind her and they forced her forward, and she had no option but to walk on, with a voice that wavered slightly on a high note, and eyes that were a brighter green than before.

The second time they passed the end of the same corridor, she cast a look of furious frustration at Luke which made her feelings plain, but he met it with stony indifference, and turned off into the men's ward, and the look he slanted at her as his voice carolled the well known

words, 'In his master's steps he trod', gave them a whole
new meaning, taunting her helplessness that would not
allow her to rebel in public.

Her voice sang on while her heart hated Luke, and
her anger was at erupting-point as they approached the
end of the children's ward corridor for the third time.
Under her breath Marion vowed fiercely, 'If Luke goes
past it this time, I'll peel off and go in there myself,
whether he likes it or not.'

Robbie would hear the singing in the distance, and
would be waiting for her to appear to sing for him as
she had promised, and she could not bear to keep him
waiting for a moment longer.

As if he sensed her imminent rebellion, Luke stopped,
and the crocodile of singers shuffled to a halt behind
him. A houseman came through the ward door and saw
them, nodded to Luke, and ducked back inside again,
and Luke told his choir, 'I think it will be better if only
a few of us sing to the children. Sister Rowley can take
in half a dozen nurses, and the rest of us will sing our
way back to the chapel and disband.'

Marion stood nonplussed, her rebellion neatly
defused by Luke's manoeuvre, and even as she waited
for the half-dozen nurses to re-form into line behind her,
Luke was already leading his depleted choir away without
a single backward glance.

'Start us off, Marion, or the little ones will think we're
never coming.'

The reminder jostled Marion back to her duties, and
in a voice that wobbled slightly to start with, she led the
way through the ward door with, 'Away in a manger,
no crib for a bed...'

They sang softly, as much a lullaby as a carol, so as
not to disturb the tinies who were already asleep. The
older children were still wide awake, and sat up in their
cots, the usually firm Ward Sister tolerant of their ex-

citement on this one night of the year, and urging Marion kindly when the singing was done, 'Go on, kiss Robbie goodnight. I know you must be longing to.'

'Oh Robbie, Robbie...' Marion hugged her small son to her. He was out of traction now, his healthy young body healing with the rapidity unique to children.

'I've been out of bed again today, Mum,' he told her what she already knew, and Marion enthused,

'Great, but don't do anything silly and risk a tumble, will you?'

This was the third day running that Robbie had been lifted out of bed, but not to walk just yet. Therapy to teach him to use his leg again was due to begin after Christmas.

'It's Christmas Day tomorrow, Mum.' Robbie's voice was suddenly mournful, and for a moment his bright cheerfulness wavered. 'I won't be at home with you for Christmas Day.'

Marion's heart twisted, but only the sudden brightening of her eyes showed her own desolation, and she ruffled the colourful curls that so matched her own, and told him briskly, 'Never mind. I'm coming to you instead.'

'Will you?' His small face brightened. 'All day?'

'Every minute of it,' she promised. 'I'll be here to give you your breakfast in the morning, and I'll be staying until after your tea party in the afternoon, and then you'll have your new toys to play with and keep you occupied. I volunteered for duty in Nurse Verity's place, so that she can be home with her family, and I can be here with you. Now, lie down and go to sleep, or Father Christmas won't come.'

She kissed Robbie again and tucked him up, and her smile was reward enough for the Ward Sister as she tiptoed out to join the other nurses waiting for her outside the door.

'I thought Mr Challoner was going to give the children a miss,' one remarked, and another, who Marion knew worked on the children's ward, answered,

'He had to wait for Dr Morgan's signal before going in. We lost a tiny yesterday.' Her young face aged momentarily with the experience of this other, dark side to her profession. 'The baby's parents came in to see Dr Morgan tonight, and it would have been too cruel to go in there carol singing while they were still in the ward office talking to him.'

It had not been spite, after all. It was Luke's natural, deep compassion that made him spare the grieving family, and she should have guessed that there must be a good reason for his missing the children's ward until the very last moment.

Instead, she had been blind, and blamed Luke, and hated him, and made her feelings unmistakably plain, and now she hated and blamed herself instead. She refused the well-meant offer from the other nurses to go and have a coffee in the canteen with them before she went home, and almost ran along the corridor towards Luke's office.

If she was lucky, she might still be in time to catch him before he left. Her conscience was a torment, racking her for her misjudgement, and driving her to make her peace with him.

What she would say to him, or how she would start to say it, she had not the faintest idea. The important thing was to find Luke before he left the hospital. His office was empty. His jacket was gone from the coat-stand in the corner, which must mean...

No summons from her emergency buzzer ever made Marion's feet fly faster than now. She sped through the doors of Casualty, ignoring the startled porter's, 'What's the hurry? Got a call-out?' and ran across the car park towards the small hospital chapel on the other side.

Chattering groups spilled out of the lighted doorway. Thank goodness, they had not all left as yet. Was Luke still among them? Her anxious eyes darted to check the parking-spaces reserved for the consultants, and her sigh of relief as she caught sight of Luke's Jaguar still in its appointed slot fogged the air in front of her as she ran.

'What's up, Marion? Trouble?' called one of the junior doctors.

Marion thought desperately, he mustn't stop me. Not now. She called back, 'No, just something I forgot to tell Luke . . . I mean, Mr Challoner.'

'I know who you mean, darlin',' grinned the young Irishman, and Marion flushed a bright red, but her need was more urgent than what he might be thinking, and she begged him, 'Have you seen him?'

Some of her urgency must have communicated itself, because the reply came promptly, 'Mr Challoner was still in the chapel when I left. I saw him talking to Mr Welsh. Oh, here he is now.'

Marion did not wait to hear any more. As Luke emerged through the chapel doorway, her feet carried her towards him as if they were guided by a radar beam.

'Luke,' she called out desperately.

So intent was she on her errand that she did not notice Michael Welsh, another of the hospital consultants, follow her quarry through the doorway.

Luke caught the sound of his name among the hubbub of departing singers, and turned an abstracted face in Marion's direction. 'Did you want something? I'll be busy for a while, so if it's not urgent . . .'

Before Marion could reply, the other consultant caught up with Luke, and resumed his former conversation. 'I know it's a risk, Challoner, but I think it's worth taking. If you could come along with me now, and have a look at the patient, I'd value your opinion.'

The two men walked away together, deep in conversation, and Marion watched them go with anguished eyes.

Did she want something?

The question bounced backwards and forwards in her brain. She wanted something now, more than she had wanted anything for many years, and like the fruit that hung above Tantalus, she knew despairingly that it would be forever out of her reach.

She wanted Luke.

She wanted him so much that she could not live without him, and knew equally clearly that she would have to learn to do just that, because Luke Challoner, eminent surgeon, and scion of one of the largest diamond-merchant and jeweller families in Europe, was not for her.

Her heart must have known of her love all along, but her mind had refused the knowledge, and now mind and heart became one, and their fusion left Marion stunned and shaking.

Her feet stayed rooted to the spot, demanding that she wait all night for Luke to return, if necessary, but some last remnants of reason that remained to her told her that it would be pointless folly to remain. Luke might be away for minutes, or it could be hours, and however long or short the time, when he did eventually turn up to claim his car, his keen mind would still be wrestling with this latest patient problem, and he would be in no mood to have his thoughts diverted by her stumbled apologies for her recent behaviour.

As if in a dream, Marion turned away from the now darkened chapel, and made her way slowly through the hospital gates to the bus stop.

The passengers were in a cheerful mood tonight, smiling and exchanging greetings with perfect strangers in the once-yearly defrosting of the habitual British reserve, and Marion smiled and replied automatically as her uniform attracted her share of the seasonal pleasantries.

Bells began to ring from a nearby church as she turned the key in her front door, but their music found no echo in her heart, which felt as empty and cold as the silent house.

She did not bother to switch on the lights. Her leaden feet carried her up the familiar stairs and into her bedroom, and the slam of the door as she shut it behind her unlocked the pent-up dam of her emotions.

With a strangled sob she threw herself face downwards on to the bed without bothering to undress, grateful for the friendly darkness that hid her collapse as she let the scalding tears flow.

CHAPTER SEVEN

MARION posted the newspaper voting-slip on her way to work the next morning.

It was still dark, and the Christmas Day streets were eerily silent as she made her way to her usual bus stop, where a special coach was waiting to pick up the hospital staff who were on duty that day.

An occasional upstairs window was already alight, indicating homes where excited children were awake early and sitting up in bed to investigate the contents of mysterious packages awaiting them.

Marion's eyes were wistful as she passed the houses, but with a determined tilt of her chin she walked on, and even managed a cheerful greeting to a wandering cat that rubbed against her leg as she paused to push the envelope containing the voting-slip into a nearby posting-box.

'Hello, puss. Are you just going out, or just coming in?'

The cat gave her a stare that said it was none of her business, and caused Marion to smile in a way she had been incapable of minutes before. She felt better, now that she had posted her vote in support of Luke. It eased her conscience a little about her behaviour towards him yesterday. That had helped, in part, to leave dark rings under her eyes this morning, not entirely hidden under the hastily applied make-up that sought to repair the ravages left by the storm of tears that still remained, darkly threatening, just under the surface of her brittle self-control.

Luke did not know that she had voted for him yet, but she would tell him as soon as they met, and explain about her lack of understanding, after which at least her mind would be at rest on that score.

Not so her heart. She had no such easy solution to offer that.

The dark hours of night were made darker still as she struggled to come to terms with the knowledge that she loved Luke, totally and without reservation. And even blacker because she knew that love could not bring her happiness a second time, because Luke did not love her.

She could count the number of times they had been out together on the fingers of one hand, and still have some left over. And each time he had invited her out it was not for the pleasure of her company, but merely in connection with the proposed bypass, when on his own admission she was useful to his cause, as a star witness because of Robbie's accident. The moment his strategy for the bypass was completed, he had dropped her like a hot potato.

Moreover, Luke's social and professional standing were both miles above her own. His wealth set him apart, and as if this were not enough, he was an eligible bachelor, whereas she was a widow with a five-year-old child.

She ignored her own dainty loveliness, and forced herself to face the facts with the courage she had learned during the last hard years.

Luke had kissed her, not once but several times, but it would be madness to allow his kisses to tempt her to bask in the sweet illusion that it was love. Her eyes closed on the pain of his kisses, but doggedly she forced them open, and obliged them to face reality.

She was not in Luke's league. Designer clothes and houses with lawns that sloped gently down to the river were things that belonged to other people, and Luke's kisses had been sheer opportunism, nothing more. Such caresses meant nothing to a man.

And everything to a woman.

Marion's heart mourned their meaning to herself, and she hugged Robbie's Christmas present to her for comfort as she reached the bus stop and boarded the coach, already almost full with its early-morning passengers.

She replied to their greetings mechanically, hardly aware of who the greeters were, or what they said, but at this early hour her abstraction caused no comment, and she sat down beside a nurse whom she knew slightly from previously shared bus journeys.

The woman asked interestedly, 'Is that a present for your little boy?'

'Eh? Oh, yes. It's a toy aerodrome.'

Would Robbie show it to Luke?

For that matter, would Luke be on duty today? The fact that he might not, that he might have done his ward rounds very early and then gone home for the rest of the day, had not occurred to her, and relief, and an aching disappointment that she might not, after all, see him today, warred inside her as she followed her colleague out of the coach at the hospital gates and hurried along the corridor to Robbie's ward.

A buzz of excited chatter greeted her as she pushed open the door of the gaily decorated room. Cots were already submerged under a sea of discarded wrapping-paper, and above the hubbub, Robbie's voice called out, 'Mum!'

His young bear-hug temporarily squeezed away Marion's black thoughts, and she returned it with interest as she said, 'Happy Christmas, poppet. Happy Christmas.'

She exclaimed over the present which Robbie pushed eagerly into her hands, wrapped with more care than expertise. 'A calendar? And you've coloured the picture on it yourself? Oh Robbie, it's lovely. You've crayoned the picture beautifully.'

'Teacher helped me. She brought it in one day, and said to keep it a secret between us.'

'She didn't say a word to me.'

'I wanted to,' Robbie admitted frankly. 'But I didn't, did I?'

His mischievous grin suggested that he might be hugging another secret to him, but wisely Marion did not press him, and confessed instead, 'I wanted to tell you about this, too.'

'Ooh, Mum, an aerodrome! It's great. Thanks!' His eyes shone, and his enthusiastic kiss dispelled any lingering doubts which Marion might have entertained about the seminar. After this, she could not possibly deny the child the trip to Holland, no matter what it might cost her personally.

Loving Luke, she shrank from the cost, which would be paid for in pain, but for today she must put that behind her. Today belonged to Robbie.

Unwittingly, appendicitis Kevin helped her. He leaned out of bed at a suicidal angle and gazed in admiration at Robbie's new toy.

'It's smashing. It's just like the real thing. Let me look.'

'You'll dive headfirst on top of it if you're not careful.' Hastily Marion pocketed her precious calendar, and scooped Robbie's next-bed neighbour back to safety. 'As soon as you've both had a bath and your breakfast, you can sit up in your chairs, and have your toys on a table between you.'

A passing member of the night staff heard her and laughed. 'We tried to get them all bathed early, but it was a losing battle until they'd opened their presents. As for breakfast, you'll be lucky if you get anything sensible down them today. They've already tucked into a mixture of chocolate buttons and jelly babies that's enough to make the dietician's hair stand on end.'

She sped on to rescue an escapee teddy bear that had been pushed through the bars of a cot by its small owner, who was now wailing broken-heartedly for the return of her new toy, and for Marion the next couple of hours passed with equal speed.

At the end of a non-stop round of bathing and feeding and making beds, she sank on to the edge of the Ward Sister's desk, and surveyed the results of her efforts with a rueful grimace.

'Phew, what a scrum! And now just look at that little girl. Her face is covered with chocolate *again*, and I bet it's all over her clean sheets, too. I've only just this second finished making her bed.'

'No use worrying today,' smiled the Ward Sister, and glanced at her fob watch. 'It'll all be chaos again soon anyway. Father Christmas is due to pay us a visit any minute now.'

'The real one's visit last night caused chaos enough,' groaned Marion. 'Who is dressing up for this one?'

Before the Ward Sister could reply, the door thrust open and a deep voice called out cheerfully,

'Happy Christmas, everybody.'

Luke! His words thrilled through Marion like an electric shock. They pricked her into convulsive action, sliding her off the desk and on to legs that were suddenly unwilling to support her, with muscles that had turned to water.

She grabbed at the edge of the wood to keep herself upright, and thought frantically, I'll slip away while he's not looking. I'll hide in the sluice room until he's gone.

At Luke's appearance, all her brave resolutions fled. The well-rehearsed words with which she intended to salve her conscience for the day before took wing, and Marion longed to follow them, but her mind seemed to freeze as well as her muscles, leaving her rooted to the spot, unable to do anything but stare at the red-robed figure with the bulging gift sack, as if he were some apparition from outer space.

A hysterical giggle shook her. What a perfect description for Father Christmas. The giggle restored her to something like normality, and gave her sufficient strength to edge cautiously along the desk, but the movement caught Luke's eye even from beneath the enveloping hood, and he turned and looked straight at her.

A white cotton-wool beard hid his scarred lip, but there was no mistaking the gentian-blue stare that arrowed her through and brought her escape attempt to nought.

It jerked to a halt her movement along the desk, and her breath caught in her throat, the noise and the bustle of the ward receding from her whirling senses, leaving only Luke, staring at her across an endless void of silence that was loud with unspoken words which could never be uttered, because the only ones that would surface in her paralysed mind were, 'I love you.'

They must never reach her lips. She must not allow herself even to think them, in Luke's presence, for fear that he might guess her secret, and trample the fragile flower of her love under his heel, scorning the tender petals that would never open into sweetly fragrant bloom. Her racing pulse made a roaring sound in her ears, and above it Marion heard the Ward Sister call, 'Give Father Christmas a clap, children.'

They clapped wildly, the older ones somewhat self-consciously, Marion noticed, and sudden compassion touched her as she watched Robbie join in. Had her small son, too, lost his sweet illusion? Had seven-year-old Kevin told him that Father Christmas was, after all, only a fairy-tale? Was this the second secret that her mother's intuition told her Robbie was still hugging to himself?

Was her little boy emerging from the protected chrysalis of his early years, and finding the experience of relinquishing his sweet illusions to the harsher realities of truth as painful as was his mother?

'I've got a present for Wendy,' Luke intoned, and dived a hand into his bag. It emerged, holding a doll-sized parcel, and a nurse carried a four-year-old up to him to collect it, cradling her charge on her lap afterwards to help unwrap the parcel.

Luke was evidently conscious that his smaller patients might find his enveloping cloak and hood intimidating, and his manner was infinitely gentle and reassuring as he dealt with each one in turn. Marion watched, fascinated, as he doled out the toys, and the eager way in which all the children afterwards held up their presents to show him. Luke liked children, and it showed in their ready response to him.

Marion remembered his wry comment, 'I'm awash with nieces and nephews,' and her heart twisted as she watched him playing happily with the little ones. He would make a wonderful father.

Robbie tore off the wrapping from his present, and called out to his mother delightedly, 'Look, its a new joined-up numbers book,' and she crossed the ward in order to admire it.

'Isn't that lovely? When you've joined up all the numbers, you'll be able to colour the pictures as well.'

Nervously she was aware of Luke slowly drawing closer to the table where Robbie and Kevin sat. He made a point of stopping to talk to each of the small patients, and it was too much to hope that he would miss out the boys.

Marion clutched the joined-up numbers book, and felt her palms grow damp and sticky against its shiny cover. To retreat was impossible, and she stood her ground with a throat that felt parched, and a tongue that stuck to the roof of her mouth, and could find no words to answer when Luke came up to the table and said, 'That's a lovely book. Is it Robbie's?'

He took it from Marion's nerveless hands, and in the exchange their fingers came into brief contact, and with her heightened awareness of him, the touch was a torment. Robbie chattered, 'Look what Mum gave me, Lu...I mean, Father Christmas.'

He grinned up at the red-robed figure in a conspiratorial fashion, and Marion thought bleakly, 'He *has* found out about Father Christmas,' and felt a little part of something inside her quietly turn over a page.

She knew it had to be, but the pages were turning too fast, and she yearned to hold them back, because with all its shadow and shine she had learned to absorb, and come to terms with, the story they unfolded so far, whereas the chapters yet to come were strange, and frightening, and she feared to read on because she knew in her heart that they could have no happy ending.

Luke hunkered down between the two boys, the better to examine the toy aerodrome, and said gravely, 'That's exactly how the planes park up at Heathrow when they're waiting for passengers to board them.'

'Will we be flying from Heathrow when we go to Holland?' Robbie's innocent question dropped like a bombshell between them. Marion flinched as if from a physical explosion and felt her throat close up, making it difficult for her to swallow, impossible to speak.

Let Luke answer, she told herself hardily. He caused the mischief in the first place. Let him get out of it now, if he could. Her expression was stony as she saw Luke glance down briefly into Robbie's enquiring face, and then his eyes, twin challenges of blue, winged to Marion's and fixed there, and he said softly, '*Will* we, Marion?'

Evading the question. Hiding under his disguise as Father Christmas, and forcing her to answer it herself, dragging out from her the words he knew she would hate to utter, that would voice her capitulation out loud, so that afterwards she would not be able to retract.

Two pairs of eyes pinpointed her. Robbie's, eager and anxious, begging her to say yes. Luke's, challenging and demanding, daring her to say no. The pressure became intolerable, tearing her in two. Through the gulf of waiting silence, Robbie began to wheedle.

'Will we, Mommy?'

Mommy... Five years old, but he knew exactly how to get his own way. Marion's heart belaboured her conscience for holding back from him, and she cracked under this final, unsportsmanlike straw.

'Yes, poppet. I expect we shall fly from Heathrow.'

'Hurray! I told you we'd be going, didn't I, Kevin? Luke said...'

Marion tried to avoid looking at Luke, but the blue eyes drew her, the glint in them a triumph that salted her bitter defeat.

'The child's a diplomat,' he murmured *sotto voce*, and ruffled Robbie's bright curls. 'I must get him to teach me how he does it.'

Marion's mouth tightened, and she thought, I've just handed Luke the best present he's had this Christmas. His own way. Through set teeth she ground out, 'I must go. I've got to help with the dinner trolley,' and she turned blindly away, and found Luke right beside her when she reached the ward door.

A small girl clutched at his robe and pleaded, 'Is Father Christmas going away, Nurse Marion? Can't he stay with us?'

'He's got lots of other little boys and girls to go and see.' Marion detached her gently, and handed her back to another, pursuing nurse, and added with a smile that she hoped did not look as forced as it felt, 'After he's finished delivering the presents here, he's got to go all the way back to Iceland for his own dinner, so we mustn't keep him, or it will get cold.'

Marion glowered at Luke's taunting look as the nurse carried her charge away, and the ward door swung shut behind them, and her glare consigned him to the snowy wastelands for ever, and the merriment in his eyes broke in a chuckle that puffed out the white cotton-wool beard.

'But I'll be back, Marion,' its owner promised softly. 'I'll be back very soon,' and drew her into his arms.

'Are you crazy? Someone will see us. Loose mmmmmm...'

White cotton wool smothered her face, blotting out her protest to an inarticulate mumble, but the lips underneath the beard were the same, and their message spelled deadly danger.

Frantically Marion balled her fists and beat at the figure underneath the scarlet robe, but for all the impression she made she might just as well have tried to beat at one of his family's diamonds.

Luke took his time before he finally released her. An endless, timeless time, of mingled agony and bliss, that left Marion panicking and furious before he finally put her away from him.

She turned on him then like a tigress, driven by a corroding fear that, in the one split second of pure bliss when their lips first met, and her own could not help but respond, they should betray her love for Luke. To cover it, she blazed, 'You must be mad. You'll start the whole hospital talking.'

'What can they say, except that I kissed Sister Rowley under the mistletoe?' White cotton-wool eyebrows rose in mockery, directing Marion's startled gaze upwards to the Druid's sprig that hung provocatively over the ward doorway. 'Just an old Christmas custom,' he taunted, and leaning down he brushed his lips lightly across hers again, and laughed, shouldered his now empty gift sack, and strode away along the corridor.

'That's him gone,' Marion ejaculated in ungrammatical relief as she returned to the ward with the weighty dinner trolley, and hoped her heightened colour would be blamed on the exertion of helping to push it and not on her brief absence with Luke.

'He'll come back to cut the cake this afternoon and join in the party. He always does,' the Ward Sister answered, and Marion's heart sank, and she thought, He meant it when he said he'd be back.

'He always gives up all his Christmas Day to the hospital,' the Sister went on conversationally. 'When he's played Father Christmas to the children, he carves the turkey on the adult wards, and then comes back here to join in the party with the little ones.'

At which time, Marion would still be on duty, and unable to avoid him.

Anticipation of Luke's return lay like a brooding storm on her mind as she coaxed minced turkey and sprouts into small mouths that were only interested in receiving the jelly and ice-cream pudding, and she collapsed into a chair with a gasp of relief when finally the last child was tucked up for a reluctant afternoon nap.

An unnatural silence descended on the ward, but the respite soon ended with visiting-time and the arrival of parents and relatives, clutching yet more parcels.

'I seem to have cleared up an avalanche of wrapping-paper already today,' grinned a young nurse as she bravely tackled the latest blizzard, and Marion smiled and predicted,

'Once the party starts, you'll be mopping up spilled trifle instead,' while her heart begged without much hope, Don't let Luke come back for the start of the party. Don't let him come until it's time to cut the cake, right at the very end.

Her eyes flew nervously to the ward door each time it opened, and as teatime drew near, and the visitors prepared to depart, her nerves grew as tight as fiddle-strings with each passing minute. She could almost hear them twang when a nurse pegged back the ward doors to facilitate the departure of the visitors, and Luke walked through them, and paused to offer words of re-assurance to each small group.

'Yes, Wendy's coming along nicely. It'll take a little time, but she is on the right road.

'Kevin will be ready to come home in a few days' time. He's made wonderful progress. I'll talk to you about discharging him when you come in next week.'

His family's diamonds could not have made a more welcome gift to the anxious parents than this, Luke's own special brand of Christmas gift that only he could offer them, and timed with the sensitivity and compassion that was so much a part of Luke the surgeon.

Why was it only Luke the man who seemed to be so diamond-hard and unfeeling when it came to his relationship with her, Marion?

Later, she watched him coax down a commendable amount of bread and butter with the trifle and iced sponge cake at teatime, envied his Solomon-like settling of the argument as to who should have the Father Christmas off the cake, by reaching up and fixing it beside the fairy on the tree for all to look at, and trembled when at last the time came to kiss Robbie goodnight, and hand over her stint to her opposite number on night shift.

Luke appeared at her side again as she left the ward and faced the final ordeal of the day, that of returning home to a completely empty house.

'I'll take you home,' he announced quietly.

'I don't need a lift. There's a special coach laid on.' The emptiness was reflected on Marion's face, and in her voice, and in the sudden, unconscious droop of her shoulders, and she felt she desperately needed a lift of the sort that only Luke could give, and that not in his car.

'It's quicker by car.'

A quicker journey meant an earlier return home, and more time to think, and to brood, and resentment stirred in Marion that Luke should be the one to twist the knife further in an already too painful wound. She protested, 'I said . . .'

'I heard what you said, and it didn't sound very convincing to me.'

She could not have convinced herself, either, Marion thought raggedly, as Luke propelled her into the passenger seat of the Jaguar, and instead of fighting him off and insisting upon boarding the coach, she found herself fastening her seat-belt, while beside her Luke did the same.

She hardly noticed the lumbering coach when they passed it and headed out of town, but she noticed quickly enough when they passed by the turning to her house. She sat up in her seat, and cried, 'You've missed the turning.'

'So I have.'

'B-but . . . you said you'd take me home.'

'I didn't say to which home.'

Enlightenment dawned, and Marion's eyes widened in consternation. 'You're not taking me to the Mill House. I'm still in uniform.'

'There's only the family at home, and they won't mind your uniform. They're used to seeing me in mine. It isn't a dinner party, or anything formal like that.' He cut short her urgent objections. 'Just a drink, and a pick-as-you-please supper, and some cheerful company.'

He had guessed. He had sensed her desolation at the prospect of returning to an empty house, and taken pity on her, and his pity rasped her more cruelly than his harshness. It set flags of scarlet humiliation flying on her cheeks, and she ground out through set teeth, 'I won't go to any supper party dressed like this. *Take me home.*'

Her morning-crisp uniform was by now a glaring advertisement of small, sticky fingers, and she squirmed inwardly as she remembered the expensive designer clothes worn by the girl she had seen from the air.

'Too late, we're already here,' Luke said, and turned the Jaguar smoothly between the tall stone pillars that guarded the long drive to the Mill House.

'I won't go in looking like this. If you refuse to take me back, I'll catch a bus.' Marion ignored his bland, 'There aren't any buses on Christmas Day,' and flung open the car door as it drew to a halt on the wide gravel sweep in front of the house. Without waiting for Luke to come and help her out, she swung her legs free, and leapt out of the car.

'I'm so glad you managed to come, Marion. I may call you Marion, mayn't I? I'm Luke's mother.' A tall, sweet-faced woman, with high-piled white hair and eyes that were a mirror image of Luke's, walked down the house steps and confronted Marion as she straightened, and she thought furiously, Luke must have engineered this. He did it deliberately, knowing how I'd feel about still being in uniform.

How she felt was sticky, grubby and crumpled, and totally embarrassed by the glaring contrast between her own clothes and those worn by the older woman. A long evening dress, in heavy figured silk, of the same lovely blue as her eyes, screamed Paris. A drift of delicate perfume spoke in the same exotic accent, and Marion's eyes went involuntarily to her jewellery.

To her surprise, Luke's mother was not wearing diamonds. A daughter of the van Zelt family, who could choose from the world's most valuable gems, chose instead to wear a single rope of pearls, admittedly flawless, and perfectly matched, and pearl studs in her tiny ears. A glance at her hands revealed only a plain wedding ring, and one other above it that was obviously an engagement ring, a single sapphire to match her lovely eyes that Luke had inherited with such devastating effect.

In spite of her wealth, Luke's mother obviously had no liking for ostentatious display, and Marion surprised herself by thinking, I like her.

Her unexpected discovery quelled her objections unspoken when her hostess invited her, in a voice as gentle as her face, 'Do come in and meet the family. We're just about to start supper. You and Luke must both be hungry, after being on duty all day.'

'Too right. Meals have been a hit-and-miss affair,' Luke put in. 'I don't know if Marion managed a meal break, but the nearest I got to food was carving the turkey for the patients.'

'Then come and make up for it now.' His mother placed an arm round Marion, and drew her through a panelled hall towards an open doorway, through which floated sounds of talk and laughter, and Marion's anger against Luke intensified as she went reluctantly with her hostess into the crowded room.

One step inside the door made her wish she could crawl under a corner of the priceless Persian carpet and disappear. A glance was enough to tell her that the guests were all garbed in the choicest that London, Paris and Rome had to offer, and they bore their clothes with the unselfconscious ease which spoke volumes for the kind of wealth that allowed them to ignore the origins of the garments.

'Come and meet my husband,' her companion urged, and at her signal a tall, spare man, an older version of Luke, but with black eyes instead of blue, broke off his conversation and took both Marion's hands in his own, and smiled, and said with warm sincerity, 'Welcome, my dear. We hoped so much you would be able to come.'

Luke must have planned it all in advance with his family, but he had not said a word about his intentions to her, Marion. He had just picked her up, and brought her, like a parcel that had no say in its own destiny, and Marion's ire rose, but there was no opportunity to vent it on Luke as she found herself being introduced to the rest of his family.

'Meet my sons, Matthew and Mark.'

Quick amusement surmounted Marion's wrath. 'Matthew, Mark, Luke...?' Her pause left a laughing question hanging in the air.

'Not very original, was it? We couldn't manage a John, so we called the next one Joanne as being the nearest to it.'

'Hello.' A smiling woman of about her own age shook hands, and took over the introductions. 'This is my younger sister, Elizabeth. Betsy to the family.'

'Call me Betsy,' the other invited with an engaging smile, and eyed Marion up and down before bursting out impulsively, 'I do love your uniform. It's just what I could do with, for when I'm in the workshop.'

'The workshop?' Marion echoed, unable to hide her surprise. She could not imagine this exquisitely dressed creature within miles of a workshop.

'I'm on Dad's design team. Brooches and things, you know.' She waved a deprecating hand. 'I'm madly envious of all those pockets in your tunic. I'm for ever losing my pencils.'

'We're all losing our manners,' chided their mother. 'Marion and Luke have just come off duty, and they need their suppers. Come along, everybody.'

A general exodus started towards the next room, and Luke took Marion's arm and steered her in that direction, and she thought helplessly, It's impossible not to like Luke's family. They're all so genuinely friendly.

It was equally impossible not to feel acutely conscious of the difference in their dress, as they joined the rest of the guests at the long buffet tables, attractively laid out with every kind of Christmas fare, behind which officiated an impressive-looking chef, and waitresses with the insignia of an exclusive catering firm on their uniforms.

Luke collected two plates and turned to Marion. 'What tempts you most?'

She thrust down an hysterical desire to answer, 'You,' and substituted hastily, 'I'm not very hungry. I managed some bits and pieces during the day.'

'I've told you, you can't live on snacks. I'll get you something sensible to eat.'

Even in this he took control, and Marion had difficulty in ironing out a frown as he eased his way through the crowd to fill their plates.

Momentarily left on her own, she had leisure to watch the other guests. Rea was not among them. She tried to tell herself that she did not care whether Rea was there or not, but her eyes darted of their own accord from one strange face to another, and gave her the news that she despised herself for wanting to learn.

As if to punish her for her lack of charity in feeling glad that the other girl was absent from the gathering, Marion's roving eyes were arrested by a framed photograph standing on top of a tall cabinet, that had evidently been pushed to the wall to make way for the buffet.

Rea's face smiled back at her. The girl was even lovelier at close quarters than she had looked from the air, and what little there had been of Marion's appetite vanished altogether.

She took the filled plate which Luke handed to her and eyed its contents with disfavour, and looked round with a hunted expression for a handy dog or a plant pot in which she might surreptitiously deposit most of it whenever Luke looked away from her.

Neither animal nor aspidistra offered itself, and Luke judged her expression accurately, and commanded, 'Eat every crumb. You'll need your energy for when Robbie comes home.'

'When ... It seems like years.'

She broke off, and Luke steered her to a small table for two near to the end of the buffet, and Marion bit hastily into a hot croissant to hide the sudden trembling of her lips. She chewed at the mouthful of bread endlessly, but dared not attempt to swallow in case the crusty morsels would not go past the hard lump in her throat and cause her to choke.

She was aware of Luke's eyes searching her face. Of a waitress hovering. Any second now, Luke would insist upon her taking another mouthful of food, and want an explanation as to why she could not swallow the first. He would be angry, and criticise, and...

He thrust a glass of sparkling white wine into her hand, and ordered her quietly, 'Drink some of this. It will help it down.'

Being with Luke was like standing in front of an X-ray machine. He read every stray thought, and each passing mood, with uncanny accuracy. Marion took a gulp of the wine, and it sent the mouthful of croissant safely on its way, and the astringent taste steadied her sufficiently to be able to utter a banal, 'The buffet looks splendid.'

'The staff are all volunteers. They're singles, and I'm told they prefer to come out like this, rather than spend Christmas Day on their own.'

Singles, on their own. Marion knew the feeling all too well, and in the middle of the crowded room, depression returned like a blanket, and was intensified when a waitress came up to Luke and said, 'There's a phone call for you, Mr Challoner. It's from the hospital.'

Instantly Luke rose with a word of thanks to the waitress, and another of apology to Marion, and left to take the call. Marion picked at her food, half hidden by the first waitress, and another who came to stand beside her, at the ready for when the supper gatherers wanted their next course. The two uniformed girls whiled away the time by chatting about their surroundings.

'It's lovely here. I'm glad I volunteered to come.'

'I came last year.'

'Was it the same?'

'More or less. Although there's another photograph on the cabinet over there, this time. The girl with the fair hair.'

'It can't be peroxide. It looks too natural. Who is she? Do you know?'

'No, I haven't seen her before. But I heard someone say she's engaged to a surgeon...yes, sir, white wine, or red?'

She broke off to attend to a guest, and the other waitress walked back to help at the buffet, and left alone, Marion felt sick. No amount of wine could force food down her now.

Luke was threading his way back through the guests towards her, and depression turned to desolation as Marion watched him come. Her guess at the reason for Rea's shopping-trip to London had been all too accurate.

Luke came up to the table and said, 'I've got to go back to the hospital.'

'Take me with you,' she begged, but he was adamant.

'Stay here and finish your meal. Matthew will bring you back when you're ready.'

She was ready now and she did not want her meal, but Luke was gone before she could argue, and it seemed a hundred years before Matthew finally came round to release her and she was able to take her leave.

'You must come again,' her hostess pressed, and Marion fixed on her smile with difficulty and answered, 'I'd love to,' and wondered what Luke's mother would think if she knew just how true that was, and the pain she felt because she knew it could never be.

Matthew seemed to know the way to her house. Had Luke primed him? she wondered, and her pride curled at the possibility. It pointed to Luke taking her home and including her in his family party as a duty, and then vanishing thankfully back to the hospital as the perfect excuse to shed his responsibility.

So she was unprepared to find the familiar grey Jaguar parked outside her house when Matthew stopped his own Rover car bumper to bumper, and jumped out to help her to alight. Marion's startled glance went from the car to the house windows as she remembered with a tremor of nervousness that she had switched off all the lights when she came out in the morning.

Lights burned now, showing clearly through the drawn curtains of the sitting-room, and black dread gripped Marion, and brought her hand up to her throat as she ran for the front door.

Robbie... Had Luke been called back to the hospital because something had happened to Robbie? He must have heard her coming, because he opened the front door, and stood framed in the lamplight from the hall, and she barely had time to wonder how he got in, and how he had got hold of her key for the purpose, when she almost collided with him in her haste to question him.

'Luke, what brings you here? Is Robbie...?'

'Robbie's fine. Everything's fine. I just stopped off on the way from the hospital to bring you your Christmas present, that's all.'

And gave her the fright of her life in the process. A jumble of fear and relief, love and anger, made Marion's head spin, and she swayed on her feet. Luke's arms came out and caught her, and held her close, and she wanted to stay cradled in their safety for ever, and must not because of Rea. She pressed away from him with an effort that threatened her senses for the second time, and blurted out, 'How did you get my key?'

'Sue lent me the one she holds for you,' he answered, and before she could voice her indignation at the exchange without her consent, he added, 'Don't you want to come in and see your Christmas present?'

The only Christmas present she wanted from Luke was one he would never offer her, and Marion's feet stumbled as he drew her with him towards the living-room.

Matthew seemed to have discreetly vanished. Marion heard a car engine start up and guessed it must be the Rover, and then Luke was thrusting open the door of the living-room, and saying in his deep, calm voice, 'Happy Christmas, Marion.'

'Happy Christmas, Mum.' A small figure bounced up and down on Marion's made-up sofa bed. 'Happy Christmas, Mum. Surprise! Surprise!'

'Robbie!' Marion's feet took wings across the room. 'You brought him home, for Christmas.' Her eyes spilled unashamed tears across her cheeks as she turned them on Luke.

'We kept it a secret, Luke 'n' me, and we didn't tell, did we?'

So this was Robbie's second secret. This was the meaning of the conspiratorial glance, and the knowing, shared smile with the disguised Father Christmas. Marion rocked her son in joyous arms, and exulted, 'Robbie, you're home,' as if she still could not believe it.

Her downbent eyes, buried in Robbie's bright curls, did not see the expression that rested in the blue watching eyes above her, and her ears missed the husky note in Luke's voice as he said, 'It's got to be a Cinderella-type Christmas present, I'm afraid. Robbie's only home until the clock strikes twelve tomorrow. No, not midnight. Noon.' He smiled. 'Then he must go back to hospital, because his therapy starts the day after, to teach him to walk again. After that, he'll be home for good,' he carefully sweetened the pill, and Marion raised a shining face to his.

'Oh, Luke, I love you for this,' she breathed.

From the depths of her joy, she was unheeding of how she phrased her words, unconscious that they, too, might hold a bitter pill, without a sweetener to offer in return.

CHAPTER EIGHT

MARION made an early New Year resolution to forget Luke.

It was impossible to cut him out of her life altogether because of her work, which was still as essential to her as it had been before. But she could, and would, cut him right out of her thoughts, she determined. For the sake of her own sanity, she must.

The gap left behind would be an empty wilderness, but she would fill it with other people, and other things. She would take up a new hobby, join a night-school class, and make new friends. She did not pause to consider how, with her erratic working-hours and a small son to care for, she hoped to achieve her ambition, but she would manage it somehow, just as she had achieved other equally impossible goals in the past.

Encouraged, she sifted through the list of night-school classes advertised in the local evening paper. Cookery was out, because nine times out of ten she would probably arrive at the class too late to start cooking the dish of the evening.

Painting? She had no talent in that direction. Perhaps languages? It would be a feather in her cap if she could attend the seminar in Amsterdam speaking at least a few sentences in Dutch. Eagerly she turned to the languages column, only to toss the newspaper aside in disgust when the only language on offer turned out to be Spanish.

She reported for duty the next day with her problem still unresolved. An ambulance driver collected Robbie for the return trip to hospital, and lowered Marion's spirits still further as she sat in the back with her son tucked in the crook of her arm. She had assumed that, as Luke had brought the child home, he would take him back again.

She knew it was unreasonable to expect the surgeon to leave his duties at the hospital during the busiest period of the day in order to do a job that the scheduled ambulance service could do equally well, but disappointment knows no reason, and the snub of his neglect gravelled Marion's feelings as she carried Robbie back to his ward.

The child was philosophical, accepting the swings of fortune's pendulum with the stoicism he had early learned from his mother, and shaming Marion now into an outward appearance of calm, when only she knew how thin was the veneer covering the raging storm inside her as she handed Robbie over to the Ward Sister.

With blurred vision she headed back towards Casualty and almost collided with Luke as he emerged from his office door.

'Sorry. I didn't see you,' she babbled, and blinked her eyes back into focus again. Her heart stopped at the sight of him, and then started to beat again at a furious rate that sent the blood thudding in her ears, and its antics jerked her words from her.

Another, white-coated man was with Luke. A stranger. Marion used him as the key to her freedom, and blurted, 'I must go...in a hurry...'

Her brave resolutions melted away under the power of a gentian-blue stare, and she needed sanctuary quickly before the effects began to show.

'Don't go, Marion.' Luke put out a hand to detain her, and the feel of his fingers curled round her arm nearly stopped her heart beating altogether. 'I want you to meet Hans. He's my opposite number from Amsterdam, and the instigator of the Flying Squad over there. I've spoken to you about Marion, Hans.'

What had he spoken of? The fact that she was a member of his team only on sufferance, until he could replace her with a suitably qualified man? That she must be watched if they were called out to a child casualty, in case she should repeat her outburst over the injured cadets?

If he had, no sign of the warnings showed in the Dutchman's expression as he held out his hand towards Marion, smiled, and said in excellent English, 'I look forward to working with you, Marion.'

Working with her? Marion's mouth went suddenly dry. Was he the replacement Luke was looking for? No, he could not be. Luke said the man was his opposite number, which must make him a surgeon too. So what? Her eyes winged to Luke's face, and he explained,

'Hans and I will be changing places for the next month or two. It's essential that we learn as much as we can about each other's methods. They are as new to the work of a flying squad as we are, and we can each learn a lot from the other.'

His words became a jumble of meaningless noise to Marion. Her mind stopped at, '. . . changing places for the next month or two.' The casual words stretched like a desert of timelessness in front of her. Luke must be going soon, or why was Hans already here? She croaked a difficult, 'When?'

'As soon as Hans is familiar with our routine. When he feels confident enough to take over, it will release me to his team in Amsterdam.'

The Range Rover only had room for three crew members. Marion's heart sank at the inevitable arithmetic. She was conscious of Luke's gaze resting on her face, reading her thoughts, and his next words confirmed that he had gauged them with deadly accuracy.

'Hans will take your place on the crew. That won't exclude you from turning out for the practice sessions, of course.'

Relegated to the reserves...

Luke was cruel. *Cruel.* Each word stabbed Marion like a dagger, and the week that followed became a torment. When the buzzer in her pocket screamed a warning, she flew to answer it, and joined in the practice sessions with the others, learning to work alongside Hans instead of Luke.

And when the Ranger Rover's flashing lights and blaring siren set the andrenalin flowing to meet a genuine call-out, she writhed under the torture of being left behind, forced to stand and watch as the vehicle took to the road without her, carrying the all-male crew which Luke coveted.

After a further week of attending practice sessions only, Marion could bear it no longer, and when the Range Rover came back from its latest call-out, she waylaid Luke in his office as Hans accompanied the patient to the operating theatre.

'Does Hans *have* to come with you on every call?' she demanded. 'The Squad has been turned out to ten calls in the last three days. Surely you could have let me come with you on at least one or two?'

'You've joined in all the practice sessions.'

'Practice sessions!' Her scorn lashed him. 'They're not the same as going on genuine call-outs, and you know it.'

'And you know the reason why I'm taking Hans with me, instead of you.'

'I know the *real* reason why you're taking him every time. You always wanted an all-male crew, and now you've got one. I hope you're satisfied.'

'I'm not complaining because you're a woman.'

The crook of his lips taunted her. His hands reached out and caught her to him, and the fire in his eyes was the reverse of complaining, but Marion was too upset to care, and with a furious twist she wrenched herself away from him.

'How like a man,' she sneered. 'Kiss a woman, and she'll do anything you want. Well, I won't. I'm a crew member, not a reserve, and I've got a right to go out on a fair share of the genuine calls.'

'Hans wants the experience.'

'Hans is a surgeon, not a junior doctor. He doesn't need to be taught his job by you.'

'You obviously need to be taught your place on the team.'

Luke's hand came out again towards her, but with a quick, cat's-paw flick of her own, Marion struck it aside, and flashed, 'My place is...' Her tongue formed the words, 'with you,' but did not dare to utter them, and finished instead, 'working on the team, not sitting on the sidelines.'

'Your place is where I say it is.'

'And where is that? Pushed out of sight, the moment someone more to your liking turns up?' Why, instead of Hans' face, did her distraught mind conjure up an image of long, flaxen hair, and designer clothes? Angrily Marion thrust it aside, and swept on, 'If that's how you feel, I might as well quit the Flying Squad and go back to working on the wards.'

What was she saying? Her heart recoiled, but her tongue drove on as if it were possessed.

'That's what you'd like me to do, isn't it? That would make it easier for you to get rid of me.'

'What either of us wants is immaterial.' His eyes became twin, glittering slits in his set face, and he grated harshly, 'The work of the Flying Squad has got to come first. Personal feelings don't count.'

'Personal feelings *do* count, whether you want them to or not. The rest of us are human.'

'Suggesting that I'm not?' The glitter took on a dangerous brightness and Marion's breath caught in her throat, but there was no going back now, and she faced him defiantly, while her heart quailed within her as he gritted, 'Do I have to prove to you that I'm human, Marion? Didn't the last time teach you anything?'

It had taught her more than she wanted to know, and when Luke took an angry step towards her, her mind cried, 'Run!' but her feet froze to the spot, and she stared at him mesmerised, unable to move as he advanced. Another half-step and his reaching hands would grasp her, and . . .

'Here's your report, Luke, and the list of replacement kit I've drawn from the stores.' A brief knock on the door heralded Bill, the driver, who nodded a cheerful, 'Hello,' to Marion as he dropped the requisite paperwork on Luke's desk and turned to the surgeon. 'Do you know how our patient's getting on? It was another motorcycle accident,' he explained in an aside to Marion, and unwittingly twisted the knife in the wound, because if she had been on call with them she would have known without Bill having to tell her.

'Hans isn't back from theatre yet,' Luke responded. 'I'll let you know when I hear from him. Hang on a minute.' He checked Bill's move towards the door. 'Now you and Marion are both here, I can let you know Hans' decision. He feels sufficiently at home with our way of working now to take over the Flying Squad as from tomorrow.'

Marion remained numbly silent, letting the shock of his words wash over her, and she left it to Bill to enquire, 'What about you, Luke?'

'I fly to Amsterdam tonight.' He swivelled an icy glance at Marion. 'So you'll get your wish to become an active member of the crew again.'

He made it sound as if she wanted him to be gone, and she shook her head dumbly when he asked, 'Any questions?'

There were endless questions, none of which could be voiced, and not one of them relevant to the Flying Squad, and she had to find the answers for herself if she was ever to come to terms with her hopeless love for Luke.

He did not try to contact her again before he left.

His absence should have helped her, but a bleak time later she had to admit that her brave resolution was not working. Not an hour went by when she did not think of Luke, and during the day, fair head instead of black working beside her was a constant, aching reminder of his absence, and her nights were haunted by the thought of him being with Rea.

Joy observed critically, 'You're losing weight. Is anything wrong?'

Life itself was wrong, but Marion denied, 'Nothing at all. I'm extra busy, that's all. I'm decorating Robbie's bedroom for when he comes home.'

Joy grumbled, 'You're much too thin already. You can't afford to lose any more weight.'

'I'll put it on again soon enough,' Marion shrugged, and drove herself to frenzied activity during her off-duty hours in the desperate hope that, if she kept her hands occupied, it might anaesthetise her mind, but all she achieved was to make her uniform smock hang even more limply upon her shrinking form, and she had to resort to using a large safety pin in order to make the waist-band of her slacks fit.

January gave way to February, and the dreary succession of days continued. Calls on the Flying Squad increased in relation to the growing severity of the weather. Temperatures remained obstinately below zero in the coldest snap the country had endured for decades, but the climate could not hope to compete with the cold that crept into Marion's heart.

For the first week or two of Luke's absence, she watched daily for the postman. Reason told her that Luke would not write to her. Why should he? Their relationship, if such it could be called, was at an all-time low when he left, and pride forbade that she should write to him. But still her eyes watched, and her heart hoped, and then turned slowly to ice as its hopes remained unrealised.

The days were busy. Hans fitted into the Flying Squad team like the last piece of a jigsaw puzzle, but although Marion liked the Dutchman, and worked easily with him, he had neither Luke's charisma nor the special driving force that made her forget her own tiredness and stress while she was working alongside him.

Now, when she went off duty each evening, she was draggingly conscious of both, and the result when she got home showed in irritability that spoiled several lengths of wallpaper and obliged her to buy another roll to match.

Hans imparted information from time to time. 'Luke is settling in well with my team in Amsterdam. Of course, he's familiar with my language, as I am with English, so he has no difficulty on that score.'

Equally, Luke appeared to have no difficulty in forgetting his own team back in England, since he sent no personal word to either of them. No doubt Rea was a major factor in helping his lapse of memory, Marion thought sourly, and flogged herself into further furious activity, vainly trying to stifle her unwelcome memories of him, until even Robbie noticed. 'You look tired, Mum. Have you had a busy day?'

Busy days, and sleepless, tormented nights, with Robbie's increasing mobility the only sweetener to help her along. Came a day when the houseman pronounced, 'You can take your little boy home tomorrow. He'll make a nice Valentine for you.'

St Valentine's Day. Marion had forgotten. Not that it made any difference to her any more. By now she had given up hope of hearing from Luke, but having Robbie home again would be the perfect antidote to brooding about the surgeon.

She took Robbie home the next day, and Luke's letter was waiting for her on the mat when she opened the front door.

It was pure coincidence that it had arrived on February the fourteenth, of course. It had to be. Nevertheless, Marion's heart pounded as she bent to pick it up.

'You're behaving like a silly teenager,' she scorned herself, and deliberately put the letter to one side, to read later after Robbie had gone to bed, and concentrated on helping her excited son to open the little pile of welcome home cards that awaited him from his small classmates.

Later, she sat upstairs with Robbie until he finally dropped off to sleep, and condemned herself for using the child as an excuse to delay opening Luke's envelope, but her self-derision could not prevent a tight band from forming round her throat as she subsided into her chair beside the fire, and stroked fingers that trembled across the familiar, bold writing which covered the single sheet of hospital notepaper.

The brevity of the letter was only equalled by the impersonal nature of its contents. They were like a direct slap in the face, and Marion winced as she read Luke's greeting.

'Marion...' Not, dear Marion. He might as well have written, Sister Rowley, she thought bleakly, and read on with eyes that blurred the bold, black script. Luke wrote, 'The exchange is working well. I've learned a lot that will be useful when I return, and so have our crews who are attending the seminar. The next course starts on April the third. I've arranged for you and Robbie to fly out on the first. Your tickets will be sent on to you direct from the travel agents. I'll meet you at the airport.'

He ended it simply, 'Luke.' The U was curved inwards slightly, as if his pen had automatically started to write,

'Love, Luke,' and then he'd remembered to whom he was writing, and had written just his name instead.

A warm, salty drop splashed on to the paper, crazing the ink. It blotted the U and completed the circle, turning it into the O she longed to see, and Marion dabbed it dry with her handkerchief. L-o-k-e was neither love, nor Luke, and longing for one without the other was as useless as reaching for the moon.

She ticked off the dates on her fingers. Another six weeks before she would see Luke again. The date of the flight seemed to spring out at her from the notepaper, as if it were written in fluorescent ink.

April the first. April Fool's Day.

She would be a fool to go, and a fool not to. Her longing to see Luke again, to hear his voice, and feel the touch of his hand on her arm, warred with the knowledge that by doing so she would only prolong her own agony.

Rather than endure another sleepless night with only her disturbed thoughts for company, Marion crept into Robbie's bedroom and curled up in an armchair beside him, and held his small hand for the comfort that only the touch of a much larger hand could give.

It was pointless to keep the news of the impending flight from her son. He had to know some time, and he deserved a reward for the plucky way in which he had surmounted gruelling therapy sessions that enabled him now to use his newly healed leg with confidence.

Besides, there were things to be done which involved Robbie, such as kitting him out for the stay in Holland. During his time in bed he had grown, and Marion was determined that he should not look like a poor relation beside the children of Luke's family.

The surgeon's postscript to his letter came as a considerable relief as regards her own clothing. Luke instructed her briefly to, 'Bring your uniform. You'll need it to wear during the day.'

Which left only the evenings. A long black skirt and an assortment of tops, with a couple of short dresses, and slacks for sightseeing if they had any time to spare, meant that her own needs were catered for from her present wardrobe, without having to dig into her scarce resources for more.

Robbie's teacher received Marion's apology for her son's further absence from school with the reassurance, 'Don't worry. Robbie's my brightest pupil. He'll soon catch up when he gets back. Staying in another country will be an education in itself. I'll ask him to write to the class, and tell them all about it. He's a very observant little boy.'

Too observant, Marion decided ruefully. As the first day of April loomed closer, the child commented on Marion's increasing nervousness, which she had congratulated herself on managing to hide from him.

'Are you frightened of flying, Mum?'

She was, but that was not the cause of her tension. And to use it as an excuse might make Robbie nervous as well, which would not be fair, so Marion lied, 'No, of course not. It's a wonderful feeling, being right up in the air, and spotting things on the ground underneath.'

'Does the thought of having to go back to school bother you?' Robbie teased.

The answer to that, too, was yes, Marion realised anxiously. If Luke attended the lectures as well, she doubted her own ability to concentrate, and groaned in spirit at the prospect of failing the end-of-course tests.

But if she used that as an excuse instead, Robbie might relate her nerves to his own transfer to a higher class when he returned to school, and be equally troubled.

Being a mother and a woman in love was an unenviable role, Marion decided wearily, and in a moment of blessed inspiration she managed to satisfy Robbie's questions with, 'There's lots to do before we go to

Holland. I'm anxious not to miss out anything, that's all.'

The only thing missing, as she steered Robbie into the departure lounge at Heathrow, was her courage. It oozed through the soles of her dainty court shoes, and left her quaking inwardly as the plane took off, and England became a dwindling speck beneath them.

Robbie was ecstatic, chattering incessantly about all the things he could see in the cloudless distance, and for once Marion was able to ignore the captain's announcement of their heart-stopping distance from the earth, in contemplation of the even greater dread of landing, and meeting Luke again.

Now the time had arrived, she wanted to turn and run. If she had been on a train, she would have got off at the next stop and cravenly turned tail. But Amsterdam was the next stop, and she was trapped until Luke set her free, and that was no freedom at all, but a cruel punishment for her heart that she had no faith it could endure, without betraying her love.

She had not heard from Luke since his one brief letter, but his sister had written to her, a charming note telling Marion that her visit was much looked forward to, and her welcome assured in their home some miles away from Amsterdam. Thoughtfully, Joanne had also enclosed a small note written by her own three children directly to Robbie, couched in much the same, if childish, terms, but the friendly missives merely served to increase Marion's apprehension.

It was good to know that Robbie would be looked after while she was attending lectures, and she accepted that she herself must have some contact with Luke's family during her stay, when she collected her son to look after him herself during off-duty hours, but she had not envisaged joining him as Joanne's guest, and the prospect filled her with dismay.

She had automatically assumed that she would be accommodated in the hospital complex, as were the other course members except, perhaps, Luke, who would doubtless be more than welcome under countless roofs in that most international of cities, and she could only hope, with the utmost fervour, that the roof he chose to shelter him would not belong to his sister.

The overhead warning lights came on, and Marion turned to attend to Robbie's seat-belt with fingers that fumbled so much, the smiling stewardess took over the task for her, while the child glued his nose to the window, exclaiming, 'Look, Mum, at all that red and yellow down there. What it it? What...?'

'They're tulips. I'll take you to see the flower farms while you're here. You'll love them.'

And then there was Luke, standing tall and dark, and more handsome, even, than she remembered him, waiting for them as they cleared Customs, and her heart loved him afresh, and wept inside her at the futility of it all.

'Luke!' Robbie caught sight of the surgeon at the same time, and ran forward, stumbling a little on a leg that was not quite used to running at speed, and Luke laughed and warned, 'Steady on,' and swung the boy high in his arms, asking him, 'How's my favourite patient?'

He did not ask Marion, 'How is my favourite nurse?' Instead, he set Robbie back on to his feet, and asked her casually, 'How was the flight?' as if he did not really want to know, and was only being polite.

He handed their luggage to a man in chauffeur's uniform and, keeping hold of Robbie's hand, he gave no indication that he even heard Marion's stilted, 'The flight was fine. No problems,' as she took the child's other hand, and followed Luke's lead to where a shining black limousine awaited their coming outside the terminal.

He remained aloof as the big car rolled effortlessly away across the flat landscape, virtually ignoring Marion, and concentrating his attention on pointing out to the child whatever he thought might interest him.

'Those windmills across there make the electricity for the nurseries. You'll see lots more of them while you're here. And herons, too. Look, that one has just caught an eel from the dyke.'

Marion curled up in her corner seat, and stared with unseeing eyes at the passing scenery. As far as Luke was concerned, the weeks of his absence had not bridged the gulf of their last quarrel.

It yawned between them still, empty and desolate, an uncrossable chasm, and her spirits felt as flat as the prairie-like fields that carpeted the view as far as the horizon, broken only by the silver ribbons of the dykes, an occasional windmill, or a remote farmhouse, its roof turned up at the ends like a classic Dutch lace cap.

Bleakly Marion faced the fact that, for Luke, the only link that had been between them was their work, and the things which sprang from it, such as the town bypass, and soon there would not even be that.

His glacial manner warned her that he had taken her empty threat to quit the Flying Squad at its face value, and it was too late to wish the words unsaid. Intuition told her that, no matter how well she might acquit herself at the seminar, when she returned to the General she would no longer be a member of Luke's team. Her relegation to the reserves would be permanent, and it was her own fault.

The warmth of Joanne's welcome was in sharp contrast to Luke's coldness, and her three flaxen-haired children greeted Marion solemnly, and then with squeals of glee hurled themselves on Luke.

'Did you go to the exhibition last night, Uncle Luke?'
'Was it good?'
'Did Rea like it?'

'I went, and it was excellent, and Rea will tell you all about it when she comes.'

'Quieten down, you three,' Joanne admonished her brood. 'Marion and Robbie have just had a long journey, and they must be tired and hungry.'

'Can Robbie have supper with us in the playroom? Please?' Three pairs of eyes switched from Joanne's face to Marion's. 'We'll mind his leg,' they wheedled.

'Go along, all of you.' Joanne shooed the four children in the direction of a motherly-looking woman who appeared in search of her charges. 'How beautifully uncomplicated life is at that age. Anyone looking at them chattering away together would think they'd been friends from the day they were born.'

'If only our own lives were so simple,' Marion agreed with feeling. She could not bring herself to look at Luke. The mere mention of Rea's name on his lips started an odd sensation inside her that, if she allowed herself to think about it, might become faintness.

Fighting it off, she turned to Joanne and managed, 'I feel a bit travel-stained.'

'Of course. I'll show you to your room, and you can freshen up. I've put Robbie in the adjoining room. I thought he might be happier near to you in a strange house. Don't worry about him now. Nanny will look after him, and if he wants you, she'll bring him straight away.'

'I might as well go up and get changed, too.' Luke tracked them up the stairs, and confirmed Marion's fears that he too was staying with Joanne. He added with a pointed deliberation that could only be aimed at herself, 'It's too late to go back to the hospital now. The relief crew will be taking over in half an hour.'

If Luke begrudged the time he spent collecting her from the airport, why did he not simply send the chauffeur for her? He need not have come himself.

Resentment at his attitude gave Marion the strength to accompany Joanne up the thickly carpeted stairway. She had no wish to be beholden to Luke for anything more than she absolutely had to, and she refused to allow him to make her feel guilty about something which he had chosen to do of his own free will.

She could feel his eyes boring into her back like red-hot coals, and to counteract their power, that felt as if it were melting her spine, she began to count the steps as she mounted, clutching at the numbers as a lifeline to hold on to her wavering senses.

One...two...three... They seemed to go on for ever. At the tenth, Luke turned away and headed for a door at the end of a short landing, and Marion went weak with relief as his eyes released her, and instantly needed them back again as her muscles turned to water, and left her to stumble with rag-doll-like lack of control when Joanne turned in the opposite direction, and opened another door, and bade her warmly, 'Make yourself at home. There's no rush. Dinner won't be for another hour. Come down when you're ready, and we can have a cup of tea and a chat before we eat.'

Alone in the luxuriously appointed room, Marion's knees finally buckled, and she sank on to the bed and buried her face in her hands.

This was going to be much harder than she had imagined. If she was reacting like this at the mere mention of Luke's taking Rea to an exhibition, how would she stay the course when he was living under the same roof, and she was bound to encounter them together?

Dinner was an ordeal. Joanne kept the flow of talk going with the ease of an accomplished hostess, ably supported by her husband. Luke's contribution to the conversation was monosyllabic, his mood lowering and uncommunicative, making it difficult for Marion to respond to Joanne's efforts.

She made a valiant attempt to do justice to the delicious food, but each forkful threatened to choke her, and when she sat, wan-faced, sipping her coffee in the drawing-room afterwards, Joanne diagnosed, 'You look shattered. Why don't you have an early night? You've got all tomorrow free before you start the seminar. I thought it would be nice if we went to see the bulb fields, and maybe visit our workshops. I'm sure you'll be interested in watching the cutters shape the diamonds.'

'I'd love that,' Marion answered, and meant it. An outing with Joanne would absolve Luke from any responsibility towards her. Perhaps he had worked that out with Joanne beforehand, for that very reason. She shrugged away the pain of the probability. Anything was better than a repeat of the ride from the airport, and after tomorrow there would be the discipline of lectures to help her through the days.

When Joanne's husband announced his intention of accompanying them the next morning, and the children's nanny appeared, as well as her charges, Marion wondered how they were all going to pack into the one car, even if it was the large black limousine which had brought her from the airport.

The answer was a minibus, drawn up at the front door. Luke stuck his head out of the driving-window, and called to Joanne, 'Where to first? Keukenhof Gardens, and then the works?' and her heart sank.

It was useless to try to keep Robbie beside her as a shield. His new friends were eager to show him all their own favourite spots in the famous gardens, and when their mother, with mistaken kindness, urged Marion to, 'Leave him to Nanny. She won't let him overtire his leg,' she had no option but to abandon herself to whatever fate the day held in store for her.

Its first blow removed her only other line of defence. Joanne slipped her arm through that of her husband, and confided with a smile, 'Pieter proposed to me in

Keukenhof, so it's always been a very special place to us. We visit it every year. This is our first time this year.'

Who could intrude upon even the most considerate host and hostess after that? Luke evidently thought the same, because he promptly tucked Marion's hand through his own arm, and suggested, 'You two lead on, and we'll follow behind. There are too many people here this morning for us to walk comfortably four abreast.'

And when Marion tried to pull her hand away and walk free, he bent his elbow sharply, trapping her hand, so that she could not release herself without a struggle, which he knew she would not attempt in public.

She glowered at him, but he ignored her silent protest, and paced after his sister, and Marion was obliged to do the same. She watched the couple in front enviously. Joanne and Pieter had so much that would be for ever out of her reach.

It was not given to many to be able to recapture the first magic of their early love in such a wonderland of colour, painted in millions of bright petals on a giant canvas of grass and water, all overhung with a canopy of green lace from the newly bursting leaves of the trees which filtered the sunshine into delicate shadows across the emerald lawns.

'It's like a fallen rainbow.' Wistfully Marion voiced her wonderment, unaware of Luke's downward glance reading her face.

For Joanne and Pieter, the past was a happy memory, the present a strong bond that held them both securely in its warm embrace, and their future scampered ahead of them, three sturdy, laughing children, who begged, 'Can we cross the lake on the stepping-stones?'

Their parents separated to help the nurse see her charges safely across the large wooden circles, cut from the girth of some enormous tree, and anchored in the water to provide a mildly adventurous path across the corner of the lake.

Luke asked Marion, 'Do you want to follow them, or would you rather stay safely on terra firma?'

Nowhere with Luke was safe for her, but at least the company of others cushioned his impact, if only slightly. His attention was partly diverted by the antics of the children, squealing with excitement as they jumped the short distance from one floating haven to the other, and his grip on her arm slackened ever so slightly, but it was sufficient for Marion.

Quick as a flash she cried, 'Why not?' and tugged her hand free, and leapt on to the first wooden circle in the water.

The distance from one to the other was only a short step, and in a trice Marion was three from the bank. Luke caught up with her on the fourth. She stood in the middle of the circle, and he landed on the very edge.

The wooden disc was designed to accommodate such touch downs, but under the additional weight of the second grown-up it moved ever so slightly, and Marion let out a gasp.

'Careful. You'll tip us both into the lake.'

Instinctively she spread her arms wide to correct the balance, and Luke's lips parted in a grin. 'I can't resist the invitation,' he murmured wickedly, and wrapped her tightly round with both of his.

The wooden disc swayed again, and fearfully Marion clung to him, and he laughed down into her face. Unable to meet his eyes, she turned her own on the water beneath them, and met instead their blue reflection, taunting her from the spreading ripples that mischievously mirrored two people locked so closely in each other's arms that their reflection became one.

'Where do we go from here?' Luke teased, and Marion swallowed convulsively. Her love was a cul de sac, leading to nowhere. But the chemistry between them was as strong as ever.

She had thought that their last quarrel must have killed it, and Luke's prolonged absence laid it to rest. The glint in his eyes told her that the fires had only been damped down, and his touch rekindled the flames that swept through her like a forest fire.

Suddenly, the colours of the flowers seemed brighter and more vibrant, and their perfume sweeter. A drift of narcissi turned the air into wine about them, a heady, intoxicating draught that made her senses reel. She closed her eyes against the dizziness, and Luke mistook her shuttered lids for fear of the water, and said, 'Hold tight. I'll carry you across the rest,' and before she realised his intention, he swept her high into his arms and jumped, sure-footed, from one miniature raft to the next.

He set her on her feet on the opposite bank, and kept his one arm round her waist, drawing her close against him as they strolled on after the others. On legs that trembled from his closeness, Marion longed to flee from his hold, and contrarily needed it as much as her heart needed him, to keep her upright.

The rest of the day passed in a daze for Marion.

The children clambered over the windmill, gazed enchanted at the baby animals housed for their delight in the children's corner, and fed a large amount of their good lunch to the flotilla of waiting swans cruising on the lake beside the restaurant.

And when afterwards Pieter said to Luke, 'The children want to go on a canal trip. We'll go with them to give Nanny a hand. We can drop you off at the cutting-house, so that Marion can see the diamonds, and one of the works cars will bring you back home,' how could she explain her blind panic at the prospect of being left alone with Luke, and beg to be allowed to go with them?

However, there were others in the cutting-house to put off the dreaded time. Craftsmen with steady eyes and even steadier hands, cutting and shaping each precious gem to its ultimate perfection. Knowledgeable girls, who used long, thin forceps to place cut gems side by side on dark velvet, so that Marion could compare their colour and quality.

'The blue-white ones are the best,' Luke explained. 'Most of our customers like to choose their gems separately, and have them individually set to their own taste.'

Which said a good deal about the bank balances of the customers, Marion reflected, as he guided her through other departments in the inner sanctum of the firm, which were out of bounds to ordinary tourists. They caught up with Betsy, busy at her drawing-board in the design section, and Luke said, 'Look after Marion for me, Bee, while I go and sort out a works car to take us home.'

'Come and have a coffee,' Betsy invited. 'I owe you something, for giving me the idea for this.' She twirled to show off the short smock which she wore, which dripped patch pockets. 'I've never been so organised,' she grinned, and added, 'D'you mind having your coffee in a mug? 'Fraid we don't run to china.'

In contrast to the glitz of the showrooms, it was all so refreshingly ordinary that it surprised Marion into a chuckle.

'Coffee in a mug will be just like home,' she accepted, and sat on a nearby stool sipping her drink while Betsy put a few finishing touches to the sketch on her drawing-board.

'Is that a matching set of jewellery?' she asked interestedly, and Betsy nodded.

'It's for an HRH. It's great fun to see our work on television on royal occasions. Gives me quite a thrill. Although I prefer something a bit plainer for everyday use myself.' Laughingly she held out her wrist, which was adorned with a modern chunky bracelet of distinctly costume jewellery origin.

A house phone beside her buzzed, and she grimaced, 'Excuse me,' and reached for the receiver. 'Hello, yes?

He's early. But of course, I'll be right along.' She turned to Marion. 'Sorry, but I'll have to leave you. It's a customer consultation. Someone wants a hand in the designing of a love-token for his lady.'

'Nice to be cherished,' Marion murmured, and did not realise how wistful she sounded. Betsy gave her a searching look, and opened her mouth as if she was going to say something, and then thought better of it and signalled to another girl who had just come into the office. 'Here's someone who will look after you until Luke gets back. She's our tame gemologist. Rea, come and meet Marion. You can practise your English on her.'

She was just as tall, just as beautiful, and her working-gear of slacks and sweater had just the same designer stamp that Marion had come to associate with the flaxen-haired girl. She felt her heart go numb as her hand was shaken, and Rea spoke to her in an attractively husky voice, 'Everyone teases me about my English, but I do try very hard. I want so much to be... how you say...?'

'Fluent?' Marion supplied the sought-after word abstractedly, her eyes caught by the glint of light from the large, solitaire diamond ring on the girl's gesticulating hand.

Luke's love-token...

'That is so. I promised myself to be—what you say—before I marry. But there is not much time. Only a few more weeks, now.'

Only a few more weeks. Pain penetrated the numbness, and became unbearable when Luke returned, and paused to admire the variety of gemstones which Rea produced for them to see.

'These are part of an exhibition we have just mounted with the other diamond centres,' Rea explained. 'We dragged Luke along to look at it, but he does not like diamonds.'

'They always seem to me to be cold, and hard. I prefer the coloured stones, myself.'

He might well be describing himself, Marion thought. The jewels winked up at her, mocking her unhappiness, and Rea protested, 'I don't agree. There's fire in the heart of every diamond. Look how mine sparkles when the light catches it.'

There was fire in Luke's heart. Marion had felt its heat. But it was a fire that scorched and burned, and reserved its gentle warmth only for the one whom he allowed to penetrate that hard, outer barrier.

That one was Rea, as evidenced by the ring on her finger. Luke had not allowed his preference for coloured stones to sway his choice when it came to her engagement ring.

To Marion's relief the chauffeur-driven car arrived for them at that moment, and Betsy came back and offered a further reprieve by begging a lift with them when Luke followed her in, a few moments later.

'I left a set of rough sketches for Pieter to look at,' she explained. 'They're a new idea of mine for a matching necklace and tiara. But I need them now to show to this new customer. He's coming back in a couple of hours, and I'll just have time to work up something presentable from the sketches for him to look at.'

She retrieved her work from the drawing-room, and apologised to Marion, 'Sorry I had to leave you at the works. But at least it gave Rea a chance to practise her English. How did she do?'

'Very well. She told me she wants to be fluent for when she gets married in a few weeks' time.'

Marion forced the words out one by one, through lips that felt stiff, deliberately testing her own endurance by speaking her pain out loud, all the while fearful lest her own fragile self-control should crack and leave her weak and weeping, confessing her love, to her eternal shame and humiliation.

Betsy smiled. 'Rea wants my youngest to be one of her bridesmaids. I don't think it's a good idea, myself.

Four-year-olds can get pretty restless during a long ceremony. The only consolation I've got is that Luke will be there to keep a stern eye on her.'

Of course Luke would be there. No wedding could be held without a bridegroom, although surely his eyes would be only on his bride? The pain increased to a pitch that made Marion want to scream, and through a wave of faintness she heard Betsy chatter on, 'Fortunately, as soon as he's handed the ring over to Hans, Luke will be free to keep the assorted infants in order, and...'

The rest of the sentence was lost to Marion. She heard her voice croak with hoarse incredulity, '*Hans* is the bridegroom? But... I thought... Luke...'

'You've got it all mixed up,' Betsy laughed. 'Luke is the best man. I think Rea has coped with the separation very well since Hans has been in England. We've tried to keep her busy. The exhibition helped. But it won't be for long now. Goodness, is that the time?' She gave a hunted look at the nearby chiming clock, and exclaimed, 'I must fly, or I'll never get these sketches finished in time. 'Bye for now.'

The door slammed shut behind her. Marion wanted to call out, 'Wait for me,' but her voice would not work. She wanted to run after Betsy, but her feet refused to move.

She felt her eyes drawn to Luke's face by something more powerful even than her pain. Against her will they rose and met a glow deep in his eyes that reminded her irresistibly of the fire in the heart of the diamonds.

The resonant echoes of the chiming clock died away, and silence washed back. Through it, Marion could hear her heart beating, drumlike in her ears. Raggedly, she wondered if Luke could hear it, too.

He moved, and his one lithe step closed the gap between them, and reaching out his hands he drew her masterfully to him.

'You have got a whole lot of things mixed up, and so have I. It's high time we straightened ourselves out,' he said.

The glow in his eyes flared to white heat, and Marion felt a tremor run through his tall frame, transmitting itself to her body in a violent trembling that forced her to lean against him for support.

Her weak capitulation finally cracked Luke's iron self-control.

'Oh Marion, my love, my heart, it's been a lifetime without you,' he told her hoarsely, and bending his head he took her lips with the desperation of a starving man snatching at life-giving food. 'Rea and Hans might have coped with being separated, but it was more than I could bear. It's been torture, not seeing you, not hearing from you . . .'

'You didn't write to me. Only the once.'

'I wrote to you every day. I poured out my heart on paper, but I dared not post the letters in case you thought I'd gone completely mad. Oh Marion, I love you, I love you,' he groaned, and cradling her bright curls between his hands, he covered her upturned face with kisses, mumbling a disjointed confession.

'Every moment I spent away from you was torture. Before Christmas, when the family firm held their annual meeting at the Mill House, and I had to be there night after night, I hated every moment because I was away from you. And then, when I did have the chance to be with you, when I took you home the night of the carol practice, I dared not stay with you. I loved you so much, I couldn't trust myself.'

'If only you'd told me then.'

'I didn't dare. When I found your wedding ring hung on a chain round your neck, I thought you wouldn't ever want anyone else in your husband's place. I fought against loving you, but it's stronger than I am, and now I can't fight any more. Oh, Marion, give me a chance,' he pleaded. 'If you'll have me, on any terms, I'll pin your rainbow back in the sky for you, and I'll never let it fall down again. I won't expect miracles from you. I know you won't ever forget your husband...'

'Hush!' Gently Marion stopped the flow of his agony with tender fingers against his lips. 'That is all in the past. Because I loved once, it doesn't mean I can't love again. Love isn't rationed. And as for my wedding ring, I'm keeping that safe for Robbie to wear when he's older. I'll have it made into a signet ring for him.'

Suddenly her weakness became strength, and her eyes shone with the joy of knowing that her sweet illusion had, magically, become glorious reality. With eager hands she pulled Luke's working face down to within reach of her lips.

'I love you,' she whispered, savouring the words that she had never dared to utter except in her dreams. They sounded so good that she repeated them, louder this time. '*I love you*. And you won't take anyone's place. You've already got a place of your very own, for ever.'

Her upturned lips sweetly offered him that place, and he stepped into it gently, hesitantly at first, and then with growing confidence, vowing with an un-Luke-like catch in his voice, 'I'll spend my life making you happy.'

A sweet time later Marion murmured mischievously, 'There's something you'll have to know first.'

'Something important?' Luke crushed her closer, convulsively, as if he were afraid that even now she might be snatched away from him.

'Mmm. Very important. I voted "yes" to your proposal for the bypass.'

'Witch!' He punished her for tormenting him. 'So long as you vote yes to my other proposal. When will you marry me?'

'It's usual to become engaged first.' Her eyes danced. 'I'll get Betsy to design a special ring for you. What are your favourite stones?'

'You don't like diamonds.'

'Have whatever you like. My choice is emeralds. These two.' He touched her green eyes lightly with his lips, and then sobered. 'Don't keep me waiting, darling. It's been too long already. Too much time wasted, and the rest of our lives isn't enough for me.' His lips impressed his urgency on her willing mouth, even as they confessed ruefully, 'I'm my own worst enemy. I shall lose the best nurse I've ever had.'

'I thought you wanted an all-male crew on the Flying Squad.'

'That was only at the beginning. You soon changed my mind for me.'

'I can still stay on,' demurely, with dancing mischief in her look.

'Is that what you really want, to carry on working?' There was pleading in his look, but a ready willingness to give her whatever it was she wanted, no matter at what cost to himself.

'What I really want...' She hesitated, suddenly shy, but reassured by the increased pressure of his arms that begged her to go on, she confessed bravely, 'I've always wanted a family. Not just an only child,' and saw from the glow that lit Luke's face that she had given him the answer he longed for. 'My training won't be wasted, with a family to care for.'

'Do you think Robbie will mind us getting married? I love the little chap. I want him to love me.'

'Robbie already worships you, ever since you taught him to play conkers without hitting his thumb. You're the father he never knew.'

Luke smiled, that crooked smile that had the power to make her pulses leap. 'Robbie is another reason why we mustn't wait too long before we get married.' He smiled at her puzzlement, and explained gravely, 'If I'm to train him up to be a conker champion, we'll all need to be living in the same house together before the autumn.'

'You are the limit!' Marion sat up on Luke's knee and glared at him indignantly. 'Teaching my son to play conkers is no good reason to rush me into marriage. *Our* son,' she corrected, and was rewarded by the brighter glow in his eyes that lit the shining path to their future.

'Will "I love you" do instead? Too much to wait?' He pulled her unresisting back against him.

' "I love you" will do nicely,' Marion agreed, and her voice slid into contented silence as his lips claimed their own.

**In April, Harlequin brings you the
world's most popular romance author**

JANET
DAILEY

No Quarter Asked

Out of print since 1974!

After the tragic death of her father, Stacy's world is shattered. She
needs to get away by herself to sort things out. She leaves behind
her boyfriend, Carter Price, who wants to marry her. However, as
soon as she arrives at her rented cabin in Texas, Cord Harris, owner
of a large ranch, seems determined to get her to leave. When Stacy
has a fall and is injured, Cord reluctantly takes her to his own ranch.
Unknown to Stacy, Carter's father has written to Cord and asked
him to keep an eye on Stacy and try to convince her to return home.
After a few weeks there, in spite of Cord's hateful treatment that
involves her working as a ranch hand and the return of Lydia, his ex-
fiancée, by the time Carter comes to escort her back, Stacy knows
that she is in love with Cord and doesn't want to go.

**Watch for *Fiesta San Antonio* in July and
For Bitter or Worse in September.**

JDA-1